THE SUNDAY TIMES BESTSELLING AUTHOR

OLLIE LOCKE

THE ISLANDS OF

FANDYE

D1103448

ISBN 978-1-5272-3302-7
Printed and bound in Great Britain
Published by Bumpindanite Press.

Editor Emily Maddick
Illustrations by Áine Gordon
Cover design by Emma Taylor

Enquiries, orders or press contact
info@theislandsoffandye.com

For Edward, India and Lettice.
May your wishes always come true.

5

THIS IS WHERE OUR STORY BEGINS...

If you were to stand on the top of the highest cliff and look out across the ocean as far as your eyes could see, you would see the horizon; that misty line that separates the earth from the sky. We all know that. But what almost nobody knows is that the horizon holds a dark secret. It's a place where evil creatures hover, hungry for children's wishes. But let's not get ahead of ourselves just yet...

For what exists *beyond* the horizon is nothing short of extraordinary. It has been kept a secret from the human world since the dawn of time. And with good reason too. For here lie The Islands of Fandye: an archipelago of magical islands beyond your wildest dreams, where unbelievable creatures live and where wishes can come true. Tortoises as big as ships, the white horses of the waves and the curious creatures of the deep, the entire fairy kingdom of Lake Adamas and, of course, the almighty Opera-Singing Whales. All these fantastical creatures and many, many more live in harmony in Fandye amongst people who may look like you and I, but all of whom have magical powers.

What you are about to read is an epic adventure about a little girl called Antigone. But before we begin, I need to take you back to a time before Antigone was even born, when a great war between good and evil was brewing over the horizon and the future of Fandye was under threat…

This is a story of courage against all odds; a tale about what happens when curiosity leads to adventure. It is a story I have never told anyone until now – but I know it is true, because I was there and I watched it all unfold with my very own eyes.

But I warn you, what you are about to read is not for the fainthearted. Sometimes it is scary and sometimes it is sad. But I will say this – when it comes to overcoming darkness, in Fandye, as in life, light always tries to find a way of shining much, much brighter.

CHAPTER ONE

When a child is born in the human world, he or she is born with their very own star that lights up the night sky. Each star watches over its child, granting his or her wishes from the day they are born, all throughout their childhood until midnight on the eve of their eighteenth birthday.

When a child makes a wish, wherever they may be, the wish zooms up over the hills, past the crashing waves of the ocean until it reaches the horizon. Once there, it shoots straight upwards towards the stars, where the wish is granted. It all sounds fairly straightforward, doesn't it? But as everyone knows, not all children's wishes come true. Because, as with all worlds (and I promise you there's more than one), for everything that is wonderful and magical across the horizon in Fandye, danger lurks not too far behind.

The darkest, tallest peak of Fandye is known as Shadow Mountain and here live the most evil of all island-dwelling creatures. It is home to hundreds of winged monsters who, when not living in their disgusting caves on the mountain, spend their time prowling the horizon looking for children's wishes to eat. These are the Bumpindanites. And if you've ever had a wish that didn't come true, well, it's because a Bumpindanite has found it and eaten it.

The self-proclaimed leader of the Bumpindanites is a terrifying and evil beast named Sorlax, who was once human. When he died many centuries ago he was transformed into a dreadful spirit who now haunts Fandye. This monstrous winged beast stands nine feet tall, dwarfing his army of Bumpindanites, who are much smaller than their leader, but are all made in his image. Bony and fanged, with grey rags hanging off their small skeletal bodies, the Bumpindanites always hunt in packs. They have talons where feet and hands once were that can pierce through skin like a knife through butter. They swoop down on prey like an eagle might ambush a rat – their powerful, puncturing claws the last thing the victim sees.

The hum and the flap of their bat-like wings and the hiss of their hunger haunts Fandye and is feared by all. But no one is more feared than Sorlax. Never far behind Sorlax is his loyal and trusty servant, Intoku. Standing at only three feet tall, Intoku has human features and walks with a limp. His sole purpose is to serve and assist his master Sorlax with whatever evil he so desires. Away from Shadow Mountain, on the other side of the islands, lies the Palace of Fandye, home of the much-loved King Zeath, ruler of Fandye. Many years ago, when the islands were a simpler place, the King ruled with his beautiful Queen Amelia.

They had three children. The first-born, Prince Benedict, was a strong and brave heir who was loved for his noble ways. While growing up, the adventurous young prince climbed everything he could, from bed posts as a child, to the palace's turrets and mountains as a teenager. Prince Benedict was tall and handsome with a head of golden hair, he was the exact image of his father when he was young. Princess Isla arrived a few years later and was simply adored by the King. With long auburn hair and big brown eyes, she was beautiful and kind and grew up to marry her childhood sweetheart, the courageous and handsome Prince Frederick. A prince from a land far away, Frederick had loved Isla since the moment he first laid eyes on her and, when he was old enough, he travelled for months across the treacherous seas to ask for her hand in marriage. Many years later, the King and Queen were blessed with a surprise; another baby son, who they named Prince Archon. Tragically, shortly after the baby prince's birth, his mother Queen Amelia died from a terrible sickness, leaving King Zeath to raise his youngest son alone.

King Zeath's heartbreak was known to all in Fandye. However, young Prince Archon grew up to be the most cherished and loved child in all of the islands. Yet the young Archon always lived in the shadow of his older brother, Prince Benedict, the heir to the kingdom.

Seventeen years passed and the elderly King Zeath's health had started to diminish. He had grown weak and frail and spent most of his days in his bed. Meanwhile, over on Shadow Mountain, Sorlax's obsession with power had taken hold. Over the years, the monster had become completely fanatical about taking over the Kingdom of Fandye. He would spend his days and nights plotting how to rid the islands of the royal bloodline, so he could claim the throne for himself and become King.

As you already know, Sorlax has his loyal army of Bumpindanites, but what I haven't told you yet is that he also has many other messengers and spies who all report to him. Have you ever felt scared upon seeing fog in the woods or down a country lane? Scared of how it engulfs the trees, suffocating everything in its path? Well, you have every reason to be fearful, because fog works for Sorlax. It is his most powerful spy, as it is able to travel over to the human world, quietly listening and reporting back every secret to its master. The fog had heard whispers from the palace that the King's only daughter, Princess Isla, had fallen pregnant and informed Sorlax of the news. And it was this exact moment that Sorlax started conjuring a most evil plan that would change Fandye forever.

CHAPTER TWO

In the Palace of Fandye, Princess Isla and her husband, Prince Frederick, were getting ready for bed. The vast chamber was exactly how you would imagine that of a prince and princess: ivory walls played host to great oil paintings of their ancestors, alongside ornate gold mirrors. A warm, gentle light emanated from a giant chandelier lit with flickering candles. Thick tapestry curtains hung at the floor-to-ceiling windows that led out onto a balcony, and in the centre of the room stood a magnificent four-poster bed.

'It's going to be terribly chilly tonight, Your Highness,' said their chambermaid Alice. 'How about I fetch you another blanket? You can't afford to get cold, not in your condition.' She smiled and gestured towards the Princess's pregnant stomach. 'Thank you for always looking out for me, dear Alice, an extra blanket would be lovely,' replied the princess. 'Come my darling, you need your rest,' Prince Frederick took his wife's hand and helped her up onto the bed.

'Do you think it's going to be a boy or a girl?' Princess Isla asked her husband as he put his hands on their unborn child. 'As long as you're both healthy, my love, I shall be happy.' The prince kissed his wife.

'I reckon it's a boy, myself,' said Alice as she re-entered the room with a thick blanket in her arms. 'He'll grow up to be a big, strapping lad, just like his father.' She winked at the prince.

Alice turned to walk out of the room. When she reached the door, she looked back at the chandelier, her eyes staring intently at the flickering lights. Then, lifting her arm, she swept the air in front of her and, in an instant, the candles magically went out and the room fell into darkness. 'Good night, Your Highnesses.'

Everyone is scared of midnight, the most unsettling point after dusk, and the royalty of Fandye are no exception. For this is the time the Bumpindanites stir and head out through the skies of Fandye to hunt for wishes on the horizon. But this night would turn out to be different. For over on the other side of the island, Sorlax's evil plan was under way, and an army of Bumpindanites were making their way from Shadow Mountain to the royal Palace of Fandye.

Isla opened her eyes, jolted from her sleep by the most feared noise in all of the islands. The Bumpindanites' screeches seemed closer than usual tonight, she thought. But Isla knew that, by her father's decree, it was forbidden for the beasts to trespass on royal property. They wouldn't dare come near, she reassured herself, as she attempted to get back to sleep.

Suddenly everything fell eerily silent. Prince Frederick remained sleeping next to Isla, as a shadowy figure passed across the balcony doors. Isla grabbed her husband's hand to wake him, as slowly the door handle started to creak and turn. Little did the princess know that on the other side of the door was more evil than she could ever have imagined.

What happened next happened so quickly that Isla didn't even get a chance to scream. The balcony doors exploded open. Every window in the turret smashed, and the bedroom was instantly swarming and crawling with Bumpindanites.

They scrambled up the walls, they destroyed the

furniture, the giant chandelier lurched dangerously to one side as three Bumpindanites swung off it. Everywhere the princess looked, the evil beasts were staring at her with bloodshot eyes, their foul stench reeking from their mouths, dribble dripping from their fangs.

Prince Frederick cowered over his wife, attempting to protect her. But the Bumpindanites had no intention of leaving without their prize.

'Be gone beasts!' bellowed the prince. But before he could muster any of his princely powers that would almost certainly kill a Bumpindanite, Prince Frederick was pinned to the bed by one of the beasts' giant wings, his entire body engulfed and his protests muzzled. Isla was hysterical. She had never known fear like this before. 'Please, please don't hurt me, I beg of you,' pleaded the princess. 'I am with child.'

But Bumpindanites care not for a child unborn, being as they are entirely devoid of compassion, or indeed any emotion other than hate or greed. Princess Isla felt an almighty claw rip through the bedsheets as the biggest beast of the pack grabbed hold of her.

An argument broke out amongst the Bumpindanites

as to who was to carry the prize back to their master and Princess Isla was tossed around the room like a rag doll, the beasts hissing and screaming as they each fought to be the one to dig their talons in. The two most monstrous beasts won and Isla was now their prisoner. Away they soared out of the balcony doors and into the night sky, the princess dangling beneath them. Behind them the entire swarm of Bumpindanites hissed in glee as they made their way home towards Shadow Mountain and to their evil leader.

CHAPTER THREE

The news of Princess Isla's kidnapping spread through Fandye like wildfire. By dawn, the islands were full of whispers as to the happenings at the palace and the fate of the princess. Some said Isla had run away, while others said a curse had been put upon her by the river pixies. But of course, all of this was just hearsay and rumour under the forest canopy. For those who knew the truth, knew that an act of war had been declared. Action had to be taken and the Princess had to be rescued.

King Zeath was utterly devastated but, due to his ill health, he had been bed-bound for some weeks and so was unable to lead the troops into battle to rescue Princess Isla. So, it fell upon the princess's older brother, Prince Benedict, and her husband, Prince Frederick, to summon an army. A mixture of men and the most magical of creatures formed the battalion. They were to set out to Shadow Mountain at the break of dawn the very next day.

Meanwhile in a filthy, slimy, wet cave high up above Fandye, Princess Isla was incarcerated. She sat in chains in the tiny space, imprisoned by rusty metal bars. Guarding her were two fat trolls with enormous greasy bellies and bulbous noses that constantly streamed with green snot. Clive and Bernard were two of the most stupid trolls you could ever come across. Constantly bickering, the brothers were armed with axes strapped to the dirty loincloths tied around their waists.

'Shouldn't have had that slug sandwich last night,' Bernard complained in his gruff tones. 'Playing havoc with me bowels.' An enormous fart trumpeted from his boily bottom – it smelt like a giant pot of boiled cabbage. 'Oi, leave it out Bernard, that stinks!' shouted his brother in disgust. 'You can't have a go at me, Clive, it's a medical problem,' Bernard retorted. 'Well stop eatin' them bleeding slugs then!' said Clive. 'Alright Bernard, shut up, the master's on his way!'

The thud of Sorlax's footsteps echoed around the cave

and the terrified trolls stood to attention. Princess Isla's prison sat at the end of a very long corridor. Hanging from the ceiling were hundreds of jars of captured fairies, their glow illuminating the cavern's rugged walls. Halfway down the corridor, Sorlax stopped and turned to an unlit jar; inside a young fairy was sleeping. The monster pressed his pointy nose up to the glass, his rancid breath causing it to steam up. He studied the tiny sleeping fairy and slowly tilted his head to one side; the other fairies trembled in fear as they watched from their own jars.

'Am I disturbing you, young fairy?' the monster

bellowed. The poor little fairy woke up and stumbling to her feet inside her glass prison, she tried to back away from his terrifying face. 'I promise you, the next time I catch you asleep I will personally pluck your wings from your tiny body little, imp,' snapped the monster. Sorlax moved on, his thudding feet heading closer to Princess Isla.

'Well, well, well, Your Highness,' Sorlax greeted her, his voice sinister and snarling. 'I must admit I have been greatly looking forward to meeting you. And what they say is true, you are pretty, just like your dead mother once was.'

While Isla was undoubtedly terrified by Sorlax, she didn't show it. But what she did reveal was her anger. The pregnant princess struggled to her feet and confronted him. 'What do you want from me?' Isla demanded as she grabbed the rusty bars of her prison cell.

'Well,' replied Sorlax. 'I'm glad you asked… I can only imagine the look on your father's face when he discovered my army had kidnapped you,' the monster laughed. 'For thousands of seasons, I have endured your family's rule of the Kingdom of Fandye. But no more. For now it is time for the Bumpindanites to rise up and for me to become King once and for all. It won't be long now until your old father arrives here to rescue you. And then I will kill him. Funny really, by you being here, you are leading him to his certain death... you must feel dreadful.' Sorlax grinned as he pressed his face up to the bars of the princess's cell.

Isla thrust her arms out in front of her body to summon her magic royal powers. But nothing happened. Instead of seeing the shafts of golden light that would have blasted the monster away, she looked down to see that her hands were covered in a sticky silver web that was blocking her magic.

'Linus dressing!' gasped Isla. She recognised the binding silk of the Goliath Hummingbird Moth that had suddenly covered all her fingers. It itched and scratched as it wriggled up to her wrists, restraining her hands.

That's right!' laughed Sorlax. 'You know that even your royal magic can't break through Linus dressing. You didn't think I would take that risk, did you?' the monster said as he turned to walk away. 'Enjoy your evening, Princess.'

CHAPTER FOUR

Sorlax had, up until this point, executed his evil plan to perfection. However, what he didn't yet know was that King Zeath was growing weaker every day and was far too sick to come to his daughter's rescue.

Back at the Palace of Fandye, as Prince Frederick and Prince Benedict assembled the troops for their mission to Shadow Mountain, crowds started to line the streets. There was a hushed sense of awe in the air, for the royalty of Fandye had never before gone to war with Sorlax and the Bumpindanites.

Up at the palace, the King summoned all his strength to leave his bed and walk through the palace halls to the bedroom where his beloved daughter had been captured. As he entered, a cold gust of wind blew the curtains through the smashed balcony doors. With tears in his eyes, the King surveyed the carnage. He looked up to see the four-clawed rip of a Bumpindanite talon scarring an oil painting. Lamps were strewn on their sides and the giant chandelier had crashed to the ground, leaving shards of glass littering the bedroom floor.

Slowly he walked to the balcony, the broken glass crushing beneath his feet. Outside the palace gates he could see the hushed crowds watching the battalion of men and magical creatures setting off to war. The King felt helpless as he watched the army depart; in all his reign, nothing had made him feel so powerless and he knew that he had failed his cherished daughter.

At that moment, a single snowflake fluttered down from the sky, past the King's eyes, and landed on his monogrammed slipper. It was a beautiful snowflake, delicate and perfectly formed. But for all its beauty, the King knew what it symbolised and terror ran through his veins.

For what you must know is that when the seasons changes in Fandye, they change in the space of one day. Winter turns to spring in a matter of hours; barren trees suddenly sprout vibrant green leaves and magnificent coloured flowers of every shape and size wriggle and twist up through the undergrowth before one's very eyes. It is the most incredible sight to behold.

But when autumn turns to winter, it is a very different story altogether. A monumental snow storm ambushes Fandye and every creature in the land retreats into hiding until the blizzard has passed. Up on the palace balcony, King Zeath knew what this lone snowflake signalled; the Great Winter Storm was coming early this year.

At the front of the vast army, mounted on horseback, Prince Frederick and Prince Benedict led the troops to battle. It would be a two-day journey from the palace to Shadow Mountain, one that would take them through the magical Forest of Pendragon, where the fairies, river pixies and imps dwell. The mission would then take the army on through the Great Clear, land of the Colossal Tortoise and on to their final destination, the most evil place in all of Fandye.

Onwards the army marched with no time for rest until they reached the base of Shadow Mountain. As they started the ascent, the hissing and the screeching of the Bumpindanites was suddenly drowned out as an almighty wind engulfed the mountain. Out of nowhere, snow started whirling and enormous boulders of frozen hail assaulted the land.

The Great Winter Storm had arrived. All the men's beards were transformed into icicles in an instant as the temperature plummeted to well below freezing. The horses reared in distress, their hooves struggling as the ground beneath them morphed into sheet ice. The snow was now pelting down, thrashing the troops from every angle. All around, the storm's whistle was deafening and, up ahead, an avalanche started rumbling down the mountain.

Prince Benedict stopped to address the battalion. 'Troops! We are in great danger,' he bellowed over the treacherous weather. 'The Great Winter Storm has come early and it is now upon us. We must double our pace and reach the summit before the ice takes hold. There is no way we can fight the Bumpindanites in these conditions.'

Just one mile and one hour later, they lost. Nature defeated them and every man, mammal and magical creature perished on Shadow Mountain.

CHAPTER FIVE

The scenes of devastation on Shadow Mountain were too upsetting to speak of. Two hundred and ninety-three souls lost their lives in one instant. Families had been torn apart, marriages destroyed. And while The Great Winter Storm may have finally subsided and the islands transformed into a tranquil and glistening winter kingdom, there was no happiness in Fandye. Fandye was in mourning.

King Zeath had lost his oldest son Benedict, his son-in-law Frederick and still no one had news as to Princess Isla's fate. The King looked back over his life and reign. Having lost his beloved Queen Amelia some seventeen years ago, he thought he had lived through the worst kind of suffering. But to lose two children and to live with the responsibility for the loss of the army of Fandye, well it had become too much for King

Zeath's frail being. And when he thought of what could have become of his beloved daughter up on Shadow Mountain, his grief was inconsolable.

The night after the tragedy on Shadow Mountain, His Majesty, King Zeath IV of Fandye, died of heartbreak shortly before midnight. When a king of Fandye dies, and exhales his last breath, all his magical kingly powers are expelled from his body. Imagine blowing out a candle and watching the smoke rise up from the wick, this is exactly what it looks like when the magical kingly powers depart the body through the hands.

The powers then drift and swirl in a golden smoke, searching through the kingdom for the heir to the throne. With Prince Benedict now dead, on this occasion it was the only remaining son, seventeen-year-old Prince Archon whose destiny was about to change forever. The young prince lay sleeping in his chamber when the powers found him. They slid under the door and crept up towards his body before entering through his mouth. The tips of Prince Archon's fingers started glowing with a golden light and soon his whole body started to glisten – the powers of his father had been transferred. The young man awoke and immediately knew he was no longer a prince. He was now His Royal Highness King

Archon I of Fandye. He ran to his father's chamber to see the former King's soulless corpse, lying peacefully on the bed.

Up until this day, Archon had been raised in the privileged life of the younger prince, watching as his elder brother Benedict was groomed to be the heir to the kingdom of Fandye. Having never known his mother, Queen Amelia, who died when he was just a baby, Archon was always treated kindly by everyone. He was a sweet, gentle and loving boy, but wholly unprepared for the great task that now lay before him.

Archon looked down over his father, the only parent he had ever known, and held his motionless hand. He knew now that he needed to summon the strength and the courage to lead his troubled kingdom forward.

The next day, for the second time in as many weeks, sombre crowds lined the streets to watch the body of King Zeath depart from the palace, surrounded by courtiers. The funeral procession made its way to the sea where Zeath's body was transferred to a boat and sailed over to the Island of Elysian, which was reserved as the final resting place for only the greatest of Fandye's souls.

With darkness, there always comes light, and as that tragic afternoon turned to dusk, an evening of celebration commenced. A fanfare sounded outside the Grand Tamarisk hall, the place of all great ceremonial events in Fandye, and the feeling in the crowds turned from sadness to hope as His Majesty King Archon I was crowned. A new chapter in Fandye's history had begun.

CHAPTER SIX

One freezing cold winter's evening, a few months after King Archon's coronation, something unimaginable took place. Some called it fate, others called it a gift from the stars but, while many of the islands' gossiping creatures will never know just what caused it to happen, it was set to be remembered as one of the most monumental events in Fandye's history.

As ruler of the stars, the sun protects the entrance to Fandye by keeping watch over the horizon and ensuring the islands are kept secret from the human world. But every now and then, whenever an eclipse takes place (that time when the moon crosses over the sun), the sun's view of the horizon becomes temporarily blocked, leaving the gates to Fandye open for humans to enter.

It just so happened that evening, on the other side of the horizon, a young woman named Lavinia had got lost at sea, off the coast of the human world. Despite the woman being a good sailor, her little boat had blown off course and reached the edge of the horizon. At that very moment, an eclipse began. The moon blocked the sun's view, leaving the gates to Fandye wide open, and Lavinia unwittingly sailed across the horizon. Little did she know the magical land she was about to enter.

In Fandye, the young King Archon had that evening taken his closest courtiers down to walk along the Beach of the Never-Setting Sun. Fandye was in the final grips of the bitterly cold winter, so all the men were wrapped up warm in their thick green velvet capes, all with royal crests embroidered in gold, their feed clad in fur-lined leather boots.

As he looked out to sea, the young King suddenly noticed the silhouette of a small boat cruising through the still waters. Mystified, the young King cautiously walked to the water's edge to investigate further. On board the boat, Archon could make out the shape of a tall hooded figure at the helm. The small boat steered its way closer to Archon, before running aground in the shallow water near to where he was standing. The courtiers surrounded Archon and brandished their swords to protect their King.

'Show yourself!' demanded the guards to the tall hooded figure. 'Please, I mean you no harm, but I am lost,' responded the scared young woman as she drew back her hood to unveil her face.

Archon had never seen anyone, or indeed anything, quite so breathtakingly beautiful in all his life. Within all of Fandye's splendour, nothing compared to the beauty of the young woman standing in front of him. Trembling both with fear and the freezing winter air, Lavinia tucked her golden hair behind her ear and asked, 'Where am I?' Her wide green eyes filled with tears as she looked at the group of men.

Archon, still awestruck by the young woman's beauty, removed his thick green velvet cape and handed it to one of his men to give to the stranger to keep her warm. 'These are the Islands of Fandye,' replied the young King. 'I am King Archon and these are my men. But more importantly, who are you and where have you come from?' 'My name is Lavinia and I was sailing when my boat suddenly changed course,' responded the young woman. 'I became lost far off the coast of

England and the tide pulled me towards a misty line. I crossed over and it led me here.' 'You are from the human world?' asked the shocked young King. Archon had never before encountered anyone from the other side of the horizon. 'May I ask please, what is your age?' 'I have just turned seventeen,' she replied.

This was not what Archon wanted to hear. And his men knew it too, as they all looked to each other anxiously. The young woman had no idea what danger she was in, being still under the age of eighteen and therefore a human wishmaker.

Now you may want to listen very carefully to what follows, as it is of great importance.

You will recall that the purity and innocence of a child's wish is the most powerful and valuable enchantment in the whole of Fandye. As you already know, when a child makes a wish in the human world, it zooms across the sea to the horizon to travel up to the stars. But that is where the Bumpindanites wait, hungry to feed off the wishes. And if a wish is eaten by a Bumpindanite, it never makes its way to the stars and this is why so many children's wishes never come true

But what you don't yet know is this: according to

ancient Fandye lore, in the islands beyond the horizon wishes can be stolen from human children and used for whatever the wish-thief desires. This ancient form of Fandye sorcery is known as extracting an 'empty wish' and it is why human children are called 'wishmakers' in Fandye. The process can only ever happen if the human child is on Fandye soil. And in theory, any creature who lives in Fandye can extract a wish from a human child. Once extracted, an 'empty wish' will always head straight to the stars and is therefore guaranteed to come true. This is why an 'empty wish' is so valuable and why a human child wishmaker is in great danger if they enter Fandye.

In the history of Fandye, such wish thievery has very rarely happened, not only because it is almost unheard of for a human child to cross the horizon, but because the process is horrifyingly painful and cruel. For when an 'empty wish' gets extracted from a human child, all his or her happiest childhood memories get wiped from their mind. It is without a doubt one of the darkest forms of Fandye magic.

Let me talk you through the process. If a wish thief decides to extract a 'blank wish' from a child, they immediately become frozen and unable to move. Then, while prizing the child's mouth open, the wish thief will slowly pincer the 'empty wish' out of the mouth with their fingers, tugging and pulling at it. The empty wish then streams out of the human child's mouth, displaying all their happiest childhood memories on a magical moving ribbon. Once extracted from the child, the 'empty wish' then becomes the property of the wish thief, who can bottle it and use it for whatever they so desire, be it evil or be it good.

Back on the Beach of the Never-Setting Sun, King Archon extended his hand to assist Lavinia to shore. 'Please, let me help you,' he said, as she stepped on to the sand. 'Thank you,' replied the beautiful young woman as she took his hand. 'You must understand that while these islands are magical, with all good comes evil and your kind is simply not safe here,' explained the King.

The young woman was undoubtedly scared, but there was something about this kind young man that she trusted. 'But how can I return home?' she asked. 'The gates of the horizon will not let you pass now,' explained Archon. 'You will have to wait until the next eclipse when the gates open again. But I promise, as I am the King, I can protect you. However, we have to keep you secret from the evil beings. You must come back to the palace with me, and you must come with me now.'

The young King Archon was fascinated with the human world and, over the next few days, he had so many questions for Lavinia. He had never met a non-magical person before, so wanted to learn everything from across the horizon to know whether the tales he had grown up hearing were true. She too wanted to know everything about the magical islands that she had found herself in.

As the weeks passed Archon used his kingly powers to ensure that Lavinia was always protected from danger and, when the King knew it was safe, he took every opportunity to show her every magical corner of his kingdom. Aside from his most trusted courtiers, the wishmaker was kept completely secret from the islands' inhabitants. The pair spent every waking moment together, sharing their secrets and dreams. It was perfect.

It had only been a matter of weeks, but Archon had fallen madly in love with Lavinia. He knew it didn't seem to make any sense, as she was from the world beyond the horizon, but when a heart is taken it knows no reason or logic. She was the most incredible creature he had ever encountered, but he knew their precious days together would soon be coming to an end. The next eclipse was looming and that was when the young woman would set sail to return home to England where she would be safe from Sorlax and the Bumpindanites. But the very thought of this happening broke Archon's young heart.

One morning, just days before the eclipse was set to occur, the King arose especially early. 'Wake up!' he whispered to the beautiful young woman lying next to him. 'I need to introduce you to someone, but we have to be quick, spring is coming!'

They mounted the King's most valiant steed. 'You must put your hood up for the journey,' said the King. 'But we won't be long.' As they galloped through the Forest of Pendragon, the snow melted underneath the horse's hooves, icicles turned to water, rivers started racing, the fairies and pixies came out of their winter hibernation and started washing in the freshly flowing streams. They headed east and, as they galloped, the branches of the forest trees started sprouting new green leaves and brightly coloured flowers began unfurling and bursting into bloom. As the forest came to an end, they arrived at an opening at the edge of a cliff and the horse abruptly ground to a halt.

'You can remove your hood now, we have arrived,' said Archon, as he helped Lavinia dismount from the steed. Directly in front of them, the young woman could see a giant clearing of land. But just as she walked towards the edge to get a better look, the ground started shaking and rumbling beneath them, Lavinia grabbed onto Archon and the horse reared. All of a sudden, an enormous daisy the size of an oak tree sprouted its way out of the land, pushing boulders of soil up into the air. And then another, and another, hundreds in fact, all whizzing up out of the ground. Then giant dandelions, even taller than the daisies, burst forth, then yellow buttercups the size of Ferris Wheels and pink and blue foxgloves as tall as skyscrapers.

The young woman looked on astonished as right before her very eyes this giant crater of land was transformed into a beautiful meadow the size of the African savanna. Spring had arrived in Fandye.

Archon smiled as he watched his love take in the spectacle. He put his hand gently on her arm and said, 'You are about to meet someone incredibly important to me. He is the oldest and wisest creature in all of Fandye and he remembers everything that has ever happened on these islands. He will not harm you, but I should tell you, he's a little bigger than you and I!'

At that moment, an enormous yawn boomed from the crater, reverberating around the rocks. The meadow flowers quivered as a reptilian foot the size of two double-decker buses stomped out of an underground den. Towering over them was one of Fandye's most revered Colossal Tortoises, who had just emerged from his winter hibernation.

'Prince Archon, Your Royal Highness, how very lovely to see you, has it been five months already?!' the colossal tortoise boomed. 'You have missed so much dear friend, I am now the King,' replied Archon. 'I am afraid we lost my father and my older brother at the beginning of winter.'

'Oh Archon! I am so dreadfully sorry,' the Colossal Tortoise bowed his gigantic neck in respect. 'Your father was one of the finest rulers this kingdom has ever known, it must have nearly been 400 years he ruled.' Archon nodded his head. 'Thank you, Timothy, it would have been 403 years this year,' replied the King.

After a long pause, the Colossal Tortoise turned his gigantic neck and peered down to see Lavinia hiding behind Archon. Her mouth was hanging open in awe, her wide eyes staring in disbelief.

'Hello, young lady,' said the Colossal Tortoise. 'I do beg your pardon, I didn't see you there. Your Majesty, who is your young companion?' Archon responded, 'Timothy, this is my friend Lavinia and I brought her here to meet you, she is a wishmaker.' Timothy's eyes slowly blinked in surprise, he peered down to get a closer look. 'How extraordinary,' mused the Colossal Tortoise. 'I always remembered wishmakers to be bigger, although I was probably a lot smaller back then.' Lavinia let out a giggle.

From inside Timothy's underground den, another

Colossal Tortoise appeared. 'What's all this talk about wishmakers?' she bellowed across the plane. 'There haven't been wishmakers in these parts in a thousand years,' she said, chuckling to herself. 'Margaret, we have visitors,' Timothy called to his wife. 'Oh!' exclaimed the lady Colossal Tortoise as she squinted in the spring sunshine. 'Royalty! How very lovely!' Her curtsy made the ground quake. 'I wish I had some fresh turnip juice to offer you!'

Lavinia stood back, too awe-struck to speak. These creatures cannot be real, she thought to herself. 'Margaret,' said Timothy. 'Archon's young friend is a wishmaker.' Margaret was astonished. 'Well, my shiny shell, an actual wishmaker here in Fandye!' she exclaimed. 'Fancy waking up to this news after all this time in hibernation. Pleased to meet you my dear.' She turned to inspect Lavinia.

'Margaret, if you don't mind, I need to speak with your husband in private,' said Archon to the lady tortoise. 'I have something very important I need to discuss with him, would you kindly look after my friend Lavinia for a moment?' 'Of course!' replied Margaret. 'It would be a pleasure!'

Archon stepped down off his horse and walked over

to Timothy, who dipped his huge neck so the young king could climb up to sit on top of his head. The pair then walked off out of earshot of Lavinia and Margaret, Archon riding so high on Timothy's head he was nearly touching the clouds. Margaret then turned to the Lavinia, 'So my love, tell me about your world, I was once told about this place called the Scotland, lots of open space apparently...'

CHAPTER SEVEN

Over on the highest, darkest peak of Fandye, amongst the caves of the Bumpindanites, Princess Isla was pacing in her small prison. Her gaunt face was ashen, her once beautiful auburn hair now stuck to the side of her face with sweat as she panted for breath. Waves of pain washed over her body causing the princess to scream out in agony. Her baby was about to arrive.

The filthy, snotty troll-guards, Clive and Bernard, were in a panic. 'Should we tell the master?' Clive asked his brother. 'How do I bleedin' know?' Bernard snapped back. 'I ain't ever seen nothin' like this before and I ain't no soddin' doctor! Just keep breathin,' Clive shouted to the princess. 'I've heard it helps at times like this.'

The lights started flickering as, up in their glass prisons, the fairies watched on in horror, fluttering their wings frantically, each one of them desperate, yet unable to help the princess.

Sorlax's most trusted servant, Intoku the dwarf, approached Isla's cell. 'What is all this screaming?' the dwarf demanded. 'Yes sir, we've been wonderin' that too,' said Bernard in a fluster. 'Now I don't know much about these sorts of things, but I think she's about to have a baby.' The princess howled a blood-curdling scream. 'Please, please set me free, for the sake of my child, please, I beg you,' she pleaded with the dwarf, before collapsing in the corner of her cell. Intoku surveyed the situation and, with uncharacteristic compassion, he said to the trolls, 'I think we might need some help here, she doesn't look well. I'll summon the master.'

Intoku reached up to the giant door on Sorlax's chamber and knocked hard three times. 'Who is it?' barked Sorlax from behind the thick iron door. 'It's only me, sir,' replied the nervous dwarf. 'What news have you, Intoku?' demanded the monster. 'Um, er, well, I'm not quite sure how to tell you this, sir, but it's the princess, you know Princess Isla, she's um…' Intoku stammered and stuttered. 'Oh, do just spit it out, will you,' Sorlax interrupted impatiently. Intoku took a deep breath and composed himself. 'Princess Isla is about to give birth, but she seems to be quite unwell, sir,' he said. And then, after a pause, he said softly, 'I think she needs our help, I think we should release her. 'She will be going nowhere,' barked Sorlax. Intoku bowed his head and averted his eyes. 'Very well, sir,' he said in a whisper.

As the dwarf turned to leave his master's chamber, Sorlax called out, 'Wait!' Intoku turned to look up at his master's face, never before had he seen it so contorted with evil. 'Listen very carefully, Intoku. When the child is born, you are to take it from her and you are to destroy it, do you understand?' For the first time in all of his service, Intoku attempted to protest his master's orders, 'But sir, I am not so sure...' Sorlax shut him down. 'Intoku, this is not a negotiation,' the monster boomed. 'This is an order. There shall be no more heirs to the throne of Fandye.' He turned his back.

By the time Intoku returned to Isla's cell, the trolls had fallen silent, all the fairies' lights had gone out, leaving only a few candles flickering, and the only sound was that of a baby crying. It was Clive who was cradling the new-born in his arms, and he presented him to the dwarf without uttering a word. Intoku looked into the cell, only to see the princess's limp, lifeless body in the corner. It was clear that Princess Isla had died.

Intoku knew what he had to do next. He had never before disobeyed Sorlax. He wrapped the tiny, crying prince up in a rag, noticing how the infant's little hands glowed golden as his royal powers started to develop. He placed the baby into a wicker basket, put on his thick black cape, and set off outside to complete his master's evil, unspeakable orders. Up in his chamber, Sorlax watched from the window to ensure his servant completed his murderous mission.

Within minutes, Intoku reached the cliff's edge, the baby in the basket had stopped crying and was now softly gurgling, his tiny eyes blinking up at the dwarf in the moonlight. He looked up to his master watching from the window. Sorlax gave him the nod and watched as Intoku dropped the basket off the cliff edge.

CHAPTER EIGHT

It was the day of the next eclipse. Both Archon and Lavinia were in sad spirits at the thought of having to say goodbye to one another. They had spent the most incredible three weeks together, but if the young woman didn't leave that night to return back to England, she would miss the opening of the gates to the horizon and she would undoubtedly be found by Sorlax and the Bumpindanites. In his head, Archon knew that his love would be safer in the human realm, but his heart had another plan.

On the beach where Lavinia had sailed into Fandye, they stood waiting for the moment when the moon would cross the sun. 'Thank you, Archon,' said the young woman as she held his hands. 'Thank you for the greatest adventure of my life, I will never forget you.'

They kissed. Archon knew now was the moment to

tell her, as he would never get another chance. 'You don't have to leave!' he said in desperation. 'I know a way you can stay!' Lavinia looked at him in startled confusion. 'What do you mean?' she replied. 'The eclipse is about to happen! It's too dangerous for me to stay here!' Archon looked deeply into his love's eyes. 'Not if you were the Queen,' he said. Lavinia was taken aback. 'But how can I be Queen? I am not of your kind,' she said in shock.

'I know it seems sudden,' said the King. 'But I also know you will make me happy for the rest of my life and that you would be the perfect Queen of Fandye. I was told by Timothy on the day that spring awoke that I must follow what my heart tells me. And this is what my heart is telling me; I need you to stay in Fandye and I need you to be my Queen.'

The moon had started creeping across the sun. Lavinia had never expected this sudden turn of events. She was overwhelmed by Archon's proposal. 'Archon, I am so sorry, my heart is broken at the thought of not being with you, I don't know what to say. You know how I feel about you,' she said fighting back tears. 'Please, you must not leave!' the king begged. 'Maybe... I mean, no,' she stuttered over her decision. 'This is all so confusing... there's no time, the eclipse is happening now!'

Lavinia was desperate, but it was her head, not her heart, that led her. 'Archon, I belong in the human world. I have my family, my friends... I have a life! But I do promise,' she said as she grabbed his hand close to her chest, 'I promise that I will see you again one day.' And with that, Archon watched as Lavinia climbed into her little boat and set sail across the horizon, back into the human world.

It is almost impossible to describe just how heartbroken the young King became after losing his love to the horizon. But he held on to her promise that she would see him again and so became certain she would return to Fandye at the next eclipse. He spent his days charting the sun and moon's movement, looking longingly out to sea, hoping and praying that his love would sail back over when the gates opened again. She had to, she had promised him, he thought to himself.

But some months later, when the day of the next eclipse eventually came and Lavinia did not return, something inside him changed. He felt betrayed by his love and obsession took hold.

Days, weeks and months passed, and young King

Archon started distancing himself from everyone and spending hours alone, refusing to speak. He became angry, his compassionate spirit replaced with bitterness, resentment and darkness. No one could get through to him. The island folk started hearing whispers that the young King was losing his mind and no one could understand why. Nobody knew the truth that it was the love lost that was driving him mad.

Up on Shadow Mountain, the fog had reported back to Sorlax the whispers of the King's state of mind. It was the talk of Fandye. But Sorlax knew that this was an opportunity for him to further his quest to become the King of Fandye himself. And Sorlax also knew there was only one creature in all of the islands who would know the reason for the King's demise.

A soaring flock of Bumpindanites took flight from Shadow Mountain, away from the darkness and headed over the Forest of Pendragon, past the freshly sprung rivers and their frolicking pixies and onwards to the sunshine of the Great Clear. The Bumpindanites' hissing and screeching filled the air as they swooped and circled, hunting for the wisest creatures in all of Fandye.

A herd of Colossal Tortoises were grazing upon the

enormous dandelions, chomping away and enjoying the fresh spring sunshine. Behind them a couple of younger tortoises were drinking the clear waters of a beautiful glistening blue lake. It was a serene and spectacular spring day at the Great Clear. But all of that changed when the Bumpindanites arrived. Within moments, the sky became dark with the evil creatures. The smaller tortoises cowered with fear. They crawled as fast as their feet would carry them to their elders, who were all huddled by a gigantic canyon rock, their necks hidden inside their giant shells as they tried to protect themselves from the predators.

The swarm of Bumpindanites parted to give way for their leader. Sorlax's giant wings came swooping down, causing the dandelions to bend in his wake, and the monster landed in the middle of the Great Clear. His wings flapped down to his sides and he stood tall, surveying the scene. It was Timothy, the eldest and wisest of the Colossal Tortoises, who stepped forward. 'What do you want from us, Sorlax? You are not welcome here,' the wise tortoise said to the leader of the Bumpindanites.

'Funny you should ask, reptile,' Sorlax responded, a wry smile twisting his grotesque features. 'Many creatures on these islands have extraordinary powers. The whales have their song and their powerful oil, and of course those river pixies have that infuriating ability to become invisible. But you giant reptiles have something that, right now, I very much desire – knowledge. You have the memory of everything that has ever happened on these islands... and we all know that knowledge is power.'

'What do you need to know, Sorlax?' Timothy asked reluctantly, aware that the swarming Bumpindanites could easily attack his family. 'I understand from whispers that the young King Archon is not the man he once was,' responded Sorlax. 'They say he paces his chambers, refusing to see or speak to anyone, obsessively watching the sea. I also understand that you, giant reptile, were the last to see him and speak with him before his mind was altered. Is that true?' 'I will not tell you anything about our King. I will not commit treason!' Timothy responded in defiance. 'Oh dear,' Sorlax sighed. 'I had a feeling you might say that.' The monster then turned and gave the nod to his army of Bumpindanites.

A fresh swarm of evil creatures appeared with chains hanging from their talons. They swooped down and muzzled Timothy. Like a horse chewing on a bit, the chains were forced between his jaws, causing the tortoise to choke and gag. His giant feet were bound. Timothy kicked and shook his head, but the Bumpindanites were too fast and nimble, tugging at the chains until the huge reptile cried out in agony, his anguish echoing around the canyon. The other tortoises looked on in horror as the noble and greatly respected Timothy was tortured.

'If you won't treat me like a gentleman, then I shall not treat you like one,' Sorlax shouted. 'Now, shall we try again, reptile? What is causing King Archon to lose his mind?' The Bumpindanites cackled and hissed as they tugged the chains tighter. Timothy writhed in agony. 'I shall never betray my King,' came his muffled response, before letting out another howl of pain. As Sorlax's fury started to simmer to the surface, he noticed the smallest tortoise standing close by, who was still at least the size of two elephants. The monster approached the youngest of Timothy's herd. 'Well, if you won't give me the information that I need, then maybe your youngest will,' he smiled. 'Now little one, will you tell me about the visit from the wishmaker?'

CHAPTER NINE

In almost no point in history has there been a meeting of good and evil in Fandye. But these were uncertain times in the islands and, over the years, as Archon's good started to fade, so too Sorlax's evil grew in power.

And so it was, one evening, Sorlax made his next move. But this time he made it alone. Minus his army of Bumpindanites, the monster took flight, heading for the Palace of Fandye. Silently, he landed just outside the giant golden gates. Slowly, he walked up to the four armed guards on patrol: 'I need to speak with the king.' The guards cowered and looked at each other in shock and disbelief. 'He's not available,' stammered one. 'Try again,' said Sorlax, before adding with uncharacteristic charm. 'Please.'

Up in his chambers the young King was hidden away

as he had been for months. In front of a roaring fire, Archon sat silently, his gaze transfixed by the dancing flames. There was a knock at the door. 'Your Majesty, you have a visitor,' announced a nervous servant. 'I have told you, I won't be seeing anyone for the foreseeable future,' the young King snapped back in response, refusing to look away from the fire. 'But Your Majesty, it is Sorlax who is here to see you,' replied the servant in fear. Archon's fingers stopped tapping on the arm of his carved wooden throne.

'I beg your pardon?' said the King. 'Sorlax is at the palace?' The servant trembled over his response, 'Yes Sir, he is at the gates.' 'Is he alone?' asked the king. 'He is, Your Majesty, there are no Bumpindanites with him.'

Archon could not believe what he was hearing. This was the monster responsible for the death of almost all of his family. Sorlax had never before set foot in the palace and the thought of his presence now, not only made Archon rage with anger, but also spelled great danger. Archon's fury made his kingly powers surge through his body, golden light glowing from his hands. 'What does he want?' Archon demanded. 'He will not say,' the servant responded. 'All he has asked is to meet with you alone.' Archon closed his eyes, his mind calculating the situation. After some moments, he looked up at his terrified servant. 'Seize any weapons he has and bind his talons,' he instructed. 'And then you may bring him up to me.'

Down at the gates, the King's instructions were obeyed. Sorlax obliged without protest, his talons were bound and he was led through the palace halls up to the King's chamber.

Man and monster, the leaders of good and evil, locked eyes for the very first time. Archon walked over from the fire and looked up, as the giant beast towered over him. 'You have some nerve, Sorlax,' he said. 'What business do you have coming here to my palace?' Sorlax was calm. 'Today, I come with no other business than to have a civil conversation with you, Your Majesty,' responded the monster in a rare display of politeness. Archon let out a sudden burst of anger. 'Where is my sister?' he shouted. 'You killed my family!'

'I did not kill your sister,' responded the monster calmly, with his head bowed, refusing to make eye contact. 'But I am afraid to tell you that she died during childbirth.' Archon took in a sharp inhalation of breath. 'And what about the infant?' Archon shouted. Sorlax paused, before meeting the King's eyes. 'I am afraid he too perished.'

Archon collapsed on his throne, grief tearing through his body and his eyes brimming with tears. 'So, why are you here?' the King demanded once again. 'Well, Your Majesty,' replied the monster. 'Your tortoise friend has given me some very interesting information about you…' Archon looked startled, completely taken aback to hear of his oldest friend's betrayal. 'The reptile told me about your visit from the human wishmaker from across the horizon' said Sorlax. 'He also told me that you have fallen in love with her, but that she has now returned to the human world. And I know that it is this that is causing your insanity.' Sorlax smiled before adding, 'with all due respect of course.'

Archon remained silent, shocked by the monster's revelations. 'I am here because I would like to propose a deal, Your Majesty,' Sorlax said. 'You may not know, but I was born of human blood. Of course, it was many centuries ago, but I do have the memory of what it is like to be in love. And I also remember the pain when love is taken from you.' Sorlax walked closer to the King, who was still slumped in his throne. 'Would you like to see your love again?' the monster taunted the king, 'For I can bring her back.' Archon listened intently.

'Do you know what my greatest secret is?' whispered Sorlax. He leant in closer to Archon. 'I can cross the horizon to the human world and so too can the creatures who work for me.' Archon was stunned. 'So, if you would like me to, I could find your love and I could bring her back to Fandye, and you could make her the queen you dream of.' For the first time in years, Archon's face changed, a glimmer of hope flashed in his desperate eyes and Sorlax knew the King was at his mercy.

'But in return, I need something from you...' continued the monster. 'Now listen carefully because I would like to make you a deal. You are now the last surviving member of the royal bloodline. You have no heir of the Kingdom of Fandye. If I bring back your love, you are sure to live a happy life together, but these are the terms of the deal. Firstly, you will never have any children and therefore, when it comes to the time of your death, the royal bloodline shall end with you. Secondly, as you have no heir, to ensure your kingly powers do not die with you, you will surrender all your royal magic to me today and I shall keep them until the day of your death, when I will use them to become the new King of Fandye myself.'

Archon stood up slowly and walked towards the arched window. He looked out to sea and towards the horizon, the very place his true love had disappeared back into the human world all those years ago. The room was silent, save for the crackle of the burning fireplace. The King knew that if he accepted the monster's evil proposition, the fate of Fandye would be changed forever. But not for the first time, Archon was led by his heart.

'Unbind his talons!' the King ordered his shocked servants. Two guards came forth and nervously released Sorlax from the ropes binding his claws. The King then turned to face the monster. 'You have yourself a deal, Sorlax,' said Archon, as he extended his hand towards him to seal the pact. His hand met Sorlax's talons and good and evil connected. King Archon's arms became illuminated with golden light, sparks flickered and fizzed from his fingers. The transferring of power had commenced. Sorlax looked down and smiled as he took a bottle from under his giant wing and pulled out the cork with his jagged, pointy teeth. The King winced as his powers surged out of his body, through his fingertips, in a stream of golden smoke and straight into the bottle. Sparks spat, shooting out splinters of flashing light. Gradually, Archon's body became weak, the colour drained from his face and, once all his powers had been taken from his body, he collapsed onto his throne.

Holding the bottle triumphantly up to the light, Sorlax then inserted the cork tightly to ensure the royal powers were secure and then placed it safely back under his wing.

He looked down at the powerless Archon. 'I'm glad you came to your senses, Your Majesty,' he snarled. And with that, he turned his back on Archon's limp body and strode towards the giant window. Sorlax stood perched on the ledge and extended his vast wings. Below him the sheer drop of the cliff gave way to the crashing sea. He turned to look at the King for one final time, before jumping and flying off into the night sky back towards Shadow Mountain.

True to his word, over the next few days, Sorlax started rounding up various creatures of Fandye to travel to the human world to hunt for Archon's lost love by air, land and sea. First, he sent the ravens who circled Shadow Mountain to patrol the skies of the human world. The birds took flight from Fandye and, the moment they crossed the horizon, their black feathers became multi-coloured as they transformed into beautiful parakeets. Thousands of the birds filled the trees of London's royal parks, from Kensington Park Gardens to Richmond. Black rabbits became filthy rats who sniffed their way through the London tube stations and the underground sewerage network to gain access to every house in the land, up through the loos in the bathrooms.

And finally, Sorlax sent for one of Fandye's most majestic creatures. In the deep waters on the other side of the islands lived the Opera-Singing Whales, whose beautiful and enchanting song can often be heard on the winds of Fandye. Now it is no easy feat to capture an Opera-Singing Whale, but everyone knows that they are the only creatures in Fandye who can pass the gates of the horizon due to their magical and much prized oil. And Sorlax knew that he needed a spy who could swim up into the centre of the human world, along the river and into the heart of the great city of London to hunt for the King's lost love.

Several weeks passed and there was no word from any of the creatures who were patrolling the human world. King Archon had summoned a servant to his chamber.

Pacing back and forth in fury, the King demanded to know what news had come from Sorlax's spies.

'So?' demanded Archon of the servant. 'What do you have to tell me?' The servant bowed his head. 'I am afraid there is no news, sir,' the servant replied. 'There should be news by now! It has been weeks! Sorlax should have found her by now!' the King shouted. 'I am sorry, sir,' stuttered the servant, 'but the creatures have yet to find her.'

Archon was consumed with fury and stormed to the open window where a lantern stood burning in the twilight. 'Where is she?' Archon howled to the horizon, his scream echoing around the islands. In his fury, the King lashed out, backhanding the beautiful golden lantern out of the window and far, far below into the crashing waves. And this, reader, is where our story really begins...

* * * * * *

We interrupt this programme with a breaking news report from central London. A whale has been spotted in the river Thames. The mammal was first reported swimming upstream outside the Houses of Parliament shortly after 11 o'clock this morning and is believed to have travelled over forty miles from the open sea. The distressed creature, estimated to be around fifty feet in length, is clearly out of its depth and is struggling in the shallow waters of the Thames. A team of experts are on hand. Samples of blood and blubber have been taken for analysis and sent to the Royal Institute of Oceanography to determine the creature's origin and species which, as of yet, cannot be identified. Crowds are now lining the embankment in their hundreds from the palace of Westminster to Albert Bridge to try and catch a glimpse of this incredible occurrence. Never in history has a whale been seen in the heart of the capital and many are now speculating as to how it might have ended up so far away from ocean waters. With time slipping away to save the creature and guide it back to safety, a massive rescue operation is now underway which, it is believed, will continue throughout the night. We will bring you the latest updates on the situation as it happens. This is Sarah Ayers reporting for the BBC in central London.

* * * * * *

CHAPTER TEN

It was the 21st of January 2006 and a little girl called Antigone was staring out of her bedroom window on Cheyne Walk in London. It was freezing cold, the kind of day when even the window sills get shocked from the first snowfall. Big Ben's hands reluctantly struck 2 o'clock, shattering the icicles that hung off them, and in the air a haunting call could be heard echoing along the embankment.

Down below her on the banks of the River Thames, Antigone noticed that a crowd had started gather and it was getting larger and larger by the minute. She watched as television crews screeched to a halt and cameramen started to hurriedly unload their equipment. Police vans and fire engines cordoned off the road and rescue boats started swarming the river. Two helicopters hovered over Albert Bridge in the unforgiving white winter sky.

Antigone watched in amazement as the scenes of chaos unfolded beneath her. Now, like most twelve-year-olds, Antigone had a most curious mind so, desperate to know what was going on, she put on her pink coat and white bobble hat and snuck out of the house.

Being only small, Antigone was just the right size to squeeze her way through the crowds and head to the end of Cadogan Pier right on the water's edge. She stretched herself up on tiptoes and leaned over the railings to get a better look at what was causing the commotion. And, like everyone else that day, she was astonished by what she saw: a gigantic whale, a magnificent creature from the deep, was lying struggling on the muddy beach, its gigantic tail slapping against the shallow, brown water.

The little girl couldn't quite believe her eyes, the only time she'd ever seen a whale was in the Natural History Museum in Kensington, her favourite place in London. But she had never seen a live whale ever before, and certainly never expected to see one in the river outside her house.

'Step back, everybody!' Antigone looked up to see a tall policeman shouting and blowing his whistle, signalling for the crowds to stop pushing onto the pier's edge. But Antigone was determined to get closer to the beautiful creature. When the policeman wasn't looking, she made her move and snuck through his legs, down the pontoon and on to the muddy shores. Surrounding the whale, a rescue operation of dozens of people was taking place. A young woman leant over the creature's dorsal fin, gently pouring water over it from a small red watering can in an attempt to keep it damp. The whale let out the most enormous sigh, spraying misty air up into the sky from its blowhole.

Antigone was now only metres away from the

mammal and she watched as the men and women tried to save it. Slowly she made her way closer to the whale until she could almost reach out and touch it. Opening its giant eye, which was easily the size of a bowling ball, the whale looked directly at the girl. Sadness and desperation flooded from its eye, Antigone could feel the pain the creature was in, but felt powerless to help. She slowly reached out to touch its silky, rubbery head and she felt a deep, almost magical connection pass between them.

And in that moment, the whale's breathing became fainter and fainter and, after one last breath, it closed its eye for the final time.

'Antigone!' a large elderly lady came bounding through the crowds down the pier, shouting for the little girl, her giant apron flapping in the wind. She barged past the tall policeman and onto the riverbank and grabbed Antigone by the hand. 'What have I told you about sneaking out, young lady?' she said angrily, before stopping in her tracks and gasping. 'Well, I never!' she exclaimed. 'It's a whale! So that's what all this fuss is about, my goodness! You don't see one of those every day.'

Like the rest of the crowds, Antigone's housekeeper

was stunned by the whale's presence in the heart of London. At that moment, the policeman came down to the beach. 'Please madam,' he said forcefully. 'You and the young girl cannot be down here, I need you to return up to the road immediately!' Antigone turned to look at the whale for one final time; the enormous creature now lay lifeless in the freezing winter afternoon.

'Now, I think it's time we move on from here,' the housekeeper said to Antigone. 'Let's get you back up to the house and into the warmth, away from all of this. Your aunt is here to see you!'

Back up at Antigone's family home, number 24a Cheyne Walk, an old royal blue Jaguar was parked outside. It was a magnificent car with shiny silver wheels and round mirrors at the front of the bonnet.

'Antigone dear,' said the housekeeper. 'Your parents have decided to extend their Caribbean cruise yet again, so I'm packing your bags as you are going to go and stay with your aunt down in Cornwall for a bit.'

Now what you should know is that Antigone hardly ever saw her parents because they were always in some exotic location, travelling the world. It's fair to say they were quite selfish parents, as they never included

Antigone in their faraway travels. Every few weeks the young girl would receive a postcard through the door from yet another country, but very rarely a phone call.

Antigone was also an only child, so spent a lot of her time alone. Unlike normal children, she didn't go to school where she could meet friends, but instead was taught from home, occasionally by her father if he happened to be in the country.

Antigone knew she had an aunt who lived in Cornwall, there was one dusty photograph on the mantelpiece in the drawing room of a very glamorous-looking lady wearing a large summer hat. However, she had never met her.

'Antigone, do come down,' the housekeeper yelled up the stairs. 'Your aunt is waiting to meet you.' The little girl walked slowly down the stairs from her bedroom, her small brown leather suitcase dragging behind her. She could hear the housekeeper pouring her aunt a drink, the ice cubes clinking on the side of the crystal glass. Upon entering the drawing room, Antigone looked up to see a tall, thin and supremely elegant lady, standing looking out of the bay window at the river. Dressed in a beautiful white coat with golden buttons, a French-looking hat, red lipstick and pearls draped around her neck, her aunt turned to greet her with the kindest smile Antigone had ever seen.

'I have waited nine years to meet you Antigone,' said her aunt, crouching down to place a kiss on her head. The hat was different, thought Antigone, and she was a bit older, but this was definitely the lady from the photograph. 'I know your parents are often away, but I promise you we are going to have the most wonderful adventure together, my darling. '

CHAPTER ELEVEN

Antigonc sat silently in the back of the car on the long drive down to Cornwall. Hardly a word had been uttered between the shy young girl and her aunt. Antigone's mind was still full with the memories of the day. She couldn't stop thinking about the whale in the Thames and the magical connection she felt thcy had shared. The car passed through Devon and, as they crossed over the Cornish border, the roads became narrower and narrower.

Overgrown bushes waved their branches manically in the wind as the car tyres screeched around corners in the rain. Finally, her aunt broke the silence. 'Antigone my darling, has anyone ever explained to you the true magic of Cornwall?' The young girl had never travelled this far out of London before. She was nervous, everything looked so very different. Antigone didn't know how to respond, so she remained quiet, blowing her warm breath against the freezing window panes, watching the droplets of condensation race each other down the glass.

'Not many people know this,' continued Antigone's aunt. 'But Cornwall was where all the magic in all of the world was very first invented.' Antigone caught her aunt's eye in the rear-view mirror for the first time. 'This was thousands of years ago,' explained her aunt. 'Back when the wind and the sea were at war and, although that is now all in the past, the magic still lives on.'

Eventually, after what seemed to take forever, the car turned down a very small road. Darkness had now fallen and the ancient windscreen wipers were squeaking frantically, trying to keep off the pelting rain, while the car's headlights were the only light in the pitch-black outside. The car came to a stop and Antigone's aunt turned the engine off outside a big gate which led to a small track along the cliff. Perched on the very edge of the cliff was an old fortress that looked like a tiny castle lookout. 'Welcome to Gorwel, darling Antigone.'

The pair dragged Antigone's suitcase along the precarious path and up to the front door of her aunt's home. Seagulls squawked overhead and Antigone could taste the salty sea air in her mouth. It was bitterly cold and the wind was blowing a gale. There was no electricity at Gorwel, so her aunt immediately started lighting the hundreds of candles positioned around the house. She handed Antigone some matches to help. The whole house smelt like a fireplace, thought Antigone as she looked around to see piles of books in every corner and pictures hanging on every wall. Moroccan rugs covered the floors and shells from the beach were piled up in bowls.

There were only two bedrooms in Gorwel and her aunt led Antigone to her small room at the top of the castle which looked out over the sea. The young girl was exhausted and later, when her aunt came up to see if she would like some supper, Antigone was already fast asleep. Her aunt smiled and pulled the blanket over her, before blowing out the candle by her bedside and kissing the her gently on the forehead.

The next morning Antigone woke to see the huge expanse of grey-blue sea outside her bedroom window. She climbed up to sit on the deep windowsill to get a better look. Some of the windows were made of colourful stained glass, like the church near her house back in London, she thought. The rain was still pelting down and the waves were crashing against the rocks at the bottom of the cliff. It was horrid weather, but it was also quite spectacular. Tempted by the smell of bacon and eggs coming up from the kitchen, Antigone ventured downstairs and was greeted by her aunt with an enormous plate of breakfast.

'Does it ever stop raining here?' Antigone complained as she sat down to eat. 'This, my darling, is Cornwall!' exclaimed her aunt. Antigone dipped her toast into her runny egg yolk and sighed. The radio was on in the background and Antigone listened as the BBC newsreader began to read a report about the whale in the Thames. She jumped up from the table and reached to turn the volume up.

'After an around-the-clock rescue effort, the whale in the river Thames died yesterday afternoon shortly after three o'clock,' read the newsreader. 'Scientists from The Royal Institute of Oceanography have reported that, despite extensive research, the mammal's origin or species can still not be identified and may well remain a mystery. This is Emily Maddox reporting for BBC Radio Cornwall.'

Her aunt turned the radio off and joined Antigone at the table. 'Darling girl, when I was your age I used to get lost on these beaches, puddle-jumping or finding adventures. It never mattered what the weather was like, so I recommend you do the same!' And so, after breakfast, Antigone put on her welly boots, coat and scarf and headed down to the beach. After an hour or so of exploring in the freezing cold, she was about to turn home when she noticed a golden object rolling in the surf. Clambering over the rocks to take a closer look, she picked it up out of the water. Rubbing off the sand and seaweed, she realised that it was an old brass lantern with what seemed to be an ornate 'F' embossed on it like a crest. At that precise moment, the heavens opened and torrential rain started pouring down again, so Antigone grabbed the lantern and scuttled back up the cliff to Gorwel Castle.

Later that night, after dinner, Antigone and her aunt sat in front of the open fire, a gramophone playing classical music in the background. Her aunt sipped on a vodka martini, while Antigone sat on the sofa and stared into the fire. A large grandfather clock struck 10 o'clock, and the spinning record came to an end. Antigone yawned. 'You must be tired darling, all this sea air makes you terribly sleepy,' said her aunt. 'Shall we head up to bed?'

Upstairs in her bedroom, Antigone changed into her nightgown and got under the bed covers and thick woollen blankets. Her aunt knocked at the door and came to sit at the edge of the bed to wish her good night. But something caught her attention and she looked towards the windowsill and to the lamp in confusion. 'Where on earth did you get that, Antigone?' she asked, as she reached to pick up the brass lantern. 'I found it down on the beach this morning,' Antigone replied.

'It looks like it's still got oil in it, shall we see if it works?' suggested her aunt. She reached for some matches from the bedside drawer and lit the lantern – sparks flew and crackled from the wick. Almost immediately, a fantastical green light burst forth from the small lantern, startling both Antigone and her aunt. The light swiftly danced from green to pink to blue, then red and orange, filling the entire bedroom. Not knowing what was happening, Antigone's aunt hurriedly turned the lamp down. The multi-colours disappeared and the flame settled at a steady blue flicker before going out altogether.

Antigone leapt out of bed. 'What was that?' she exclaimed excitedly. 'I really don't know, darling,' her confused aunt replied as she looked at the now extinguished lantern. Unsure of what to say next to the curious, wide-eyed little girl, her aunt simply said, 'Let's leave it for tonight, shall we?' She tucked Antigone back into bed, placed the lantern back on the windowsill and kissed her good night.

CHAPTER TWELVE

A few hours later, just after midnight, Antigone awoke and sat bolt upright in bed as a flash of lightning struck the rocks below the cliff. She went to the window and saw that the sea and sky seemed to be angrily fighting, just as her aunt had said they once did. Lightning struck again, then a furious clap of thunder bellowed.

Inside the lantern on the windowsill, the lights started flickering once again, glowing a brighter and brighter green as they lit up the room. Antigone stared out of the window, transfixed by the line that separates the sky from the sea. Just like the lights inside the lantern, there seemed to be a wild array of beautiful, fantastical colours dancing and darting far off on the horizon. The young girl became hypnotised by the magical lights.

She'd never seen anything so beautiful in all her twelve years, she knew she needed to get closer.

Now, as we all know, curiosity can be a very dangerous game, and this set of circumstances would prove to be no exception. Antigone was drawn towards the lights, such was the power of their beauty. She grabbed the lantern and, dressed only in her cotton nightgown, headed out into the stormy night. She wound down the cliff path, the lantern leading the way. Moored on the rocks far below, glistening in the moonlight, Antigone saw a small old wooden boat with a ripped white sail flapping in the wind. She waded through the overgrown weeds, stinging nettles biting at her ankles. The freezing water lapped at her toes as she clambered across the rocks towards the tiny dinghy. But Antigone felt no pain or fear, all she knew was she had to find out where the lights were coming from. The lantern was still glowing and darting, willing her towards the horizon. She reached the boat and, without a second thought, she climbed aboard and hung the lantern at the hull. At the bottom of the boat lay two old wooden oars which she used to push the small vessel off into the sea and towards the horizon. Led by the dancing lights of her lantern, a force beyond her control was driving her forward towards the mesmerising lights.

Back at Gorwel, her aunt was startled from her sleep by the large wooden front door banging in the wind. She ran upstairs to Antigone's bedroom, only to be confronted with an empty bed. 'Antigone!' she shouted, but to no response. Over on the window ledge, a ring of oil marked the spot where the lantern had stood. But just as her terror started to take hold, the aunt, like Antigone before her, became mesmerised by the beautiful sight on the horizon. And then she saw a small boat heading in the direction of the incredible lights, a lantern swinging at its helm. She raced outside, but her anguished screams for the young girl were drowned out by the voice of the howling wind.

The white-tipped waves relentlessly crashed into Antigone's boat as if hundreds of lost ocean souls were trying to climb aboard and take refuge. A monumental crack of thunder rattled the night sky and Antigone was momentarily startled out of her hypnosis. Panicked and freezing, the little girl realised the grave error she'd made. She knew she was in great danger, that she was out of her depth, and she longed to be back in the safety of her warm bed at Gorwel. But the colours of the horizon were tantalising her ever closer.

Antigone was fast approaching the whizzing, whirling rainbow cyclone. The horizontal lights were leaping erratically like a box of fireworks that had been lit all at once. Although the storm had ripped the little boat's sail even more, somehow the vessel still moved forward. The edge of the sky loomed larger, until it appeared like a colossal wall of multi-coloured mist, towering ten times taller than a house over Antigone.

Now you have to remember that humans are never meant to visit the gates of the horizon, being kept, as they always have been, just a few miles away. But Antigone was never destined to be a normal little girl. The giant wall of rainbow mist engulfed her, she could taste it and smell it. Antigone was spellbound, she turned for a final time and looked back towards where she had come from and all that was familiar to her. She could see Gorwel in the far distance, a silent silhouette on the edge of the cliff. And in that moment, she was no longer afraid. She closed her eyes and let the lantern guide her across the horizon.

Antigone blinked, all around her was silence. The water below was now as still as a millpond. It was no longer the dead of night; instead, the sun was setting orange and pink on a land that was, quite clearly, not

England. The stars had already made an appearance here. But these stars seemed closer than any she'd ever seen before, bigger and brighter, their twinkles reflected in the ripples of the water as the boat glided towards the shore.

Far off in the distance, Antigone heard the faint call of opera on the wind; tens of voices all singing beautiful, haunting arias. It was no longer cold in this new land and Antigone breathed in the warm, tropical air. A flamboyance of fantastical flamingos glided past her, making their way towards a giant mountain range. Antigone looked up and noted that one mountain stood out far darker than the rest, hundreds of giant bat-like creatures swirling around its peak. Ahead of her, beyond the beach, she saw a beautiful forest of every kind of tree imaginable. They were all entwined with green vines covered in giant leaves and flowers sprouted from their trunks in every colour. In front of Antigone on the beach, hundreds of tiny glowing hermit crabs raced around, hiding behind enormous shells and starfish.

As her tiny battered boat hit the sandy shore, little did Antigone know that this island was alive with gossip and curiosity at her arrival. Eyes peered out from behind trees, shapes started to stir in bushes and burrows and the sea brimmed with creatures of the deep, all watching the human enter their magical world.

Antigone had arrived in the Islands of Fandye.

CHAPTER THIRTEEN

That evening, Sorlax was dining in his chamber up on Shadow Mountain, a giant feast laid out in front of him of raw dodo carcasses, slabs of whale flesh and whole live rabbits. The monster was ravenously devouring the food, ripping the flesh with his pointed fangs as his servant Intoku watched on. In the centre of the table sat the precious bottle of King Archon's royal powers, which Sorlax had extracted from him as part of their evil pact. It had been weeks since the monster had promised to find Archon's lost love, but as yet not one of his creatures had returned from beyond the horizon with any news.

Suddenly something caught Sorlax's eye. Dropping a dodo leg down on to the table, he stopped dead and stared out of the window. His eyes sharpened and his pupils shrank. He pushed the table to one side, the plates of food clattering to the floor, and rushed over to the window.

He stared in disbelief, as far out on the horizon, he saw an unusual bright green light flickering from a lantern at the front of a tiny boat. 'Come here, Intoku!' he shouted to his servant. 'Could it be her?' he asked as he pointed out the window. 'Has she finally returned?' Intoku looked out to sea as the small boat sailed closer to the shore. 'No Master, that is not the King's love,' he replied. 'That is a child...'

A sinister smile broke across Sorlax's face. 'Find her!' he demanded. 'And bring her to me.'

High up in the Forest of Pendragon a fairy was resting on a large tropical leaf, watching over the Beach of the Never-Setting Sun, when she saw quite an unusual sight. As the mist parted, it gave way to reveal a lone boat that was sailing away from the horizon and through the still waters of Fandye. The fairy watched in amazement as the tiny vessel approached the beach. She could just about make out a small figure and a lantern hanging off the front of the boat. All around her, the forest started to rustle and stir with curious activity. Wings flapped and creatures whispered – even the flowers turned their petalled heads towards the visitor on the beach.

The little fairy knew immediately what she needed to do and took flight through the treetops and down through the undergrowth until she reached Lake Adamas, home of the fairies. Amongst the thousands of fairies of Adamas, a young boy named Otto lived. That evening, he was playing in the lake's shallows with two of his closest fairy friends when the messenger from the forest arrived with the news.

With a sense of urgency on her face, the small fairy tugged at Otto's hair, her tiny hand the size of his little fingernail, and she beckoned for him to follow her. Barely the size of Otto's nose, she hovered in front of his face as she led him away from the lake, back through the forest and down to the Beach of the Never-Setting Sun. As they climbed through the mangroves at the edge of the beach, it suddenly became clear to Otto why the little fairy had led him there. For on the shoreline, in a small boat with a ripped white sail, was a human child. Otto was stunned at the sight of a human wishmaker in Fandye.

He had only ever heard rumours of the humans who lived beyond the horizon and had never seen one before. 'Pssst, turn off your lantern,' he whispered to the wishmaker. Antigone stopped suddenly and looked all around her, terrified. 'Who said that?' she asked into the dusky darkness, her lantern casting a green flare on to the sand beneath her. Otto then ran out of the mangroves towards the young girl and the beached boat.

'You must turn that lantern out or they will see you!' he said. 'Who will see me?' Antigone asked, confused and scared by the little boy. Otto put his hands either side of Antigone's lantern and the green light was immediately extinguished. 'You are in great danger,' he said to her. 'You must come with me.' Antigone, still confused, asked, 'Danger from what?' 'We have no time for me to explain,' he replied. But Antigone remained suspicious, 'Who are you? How can I know I can trust you?' she asked. 'I don't think you've got a choice,' Otto replied, before reaching out for Antigone's boat and dragging it up the sand towards the entrance to the Forest of Pendragon. Antigone helped the boy with her boat and they hid it from sight in the reeds near the woodland's edge.

'Here, take my hand,' Otto extended his arm to Antigone and they ran into the Forest of Pendragon. As they entered, still running, Antigone noticed that the trees seemed to step aside to make way for them, as if they were alive, bending to create a direct pathway through the dense maze of forestry. She looked back over her shoulder and saw that, just as the trunks had moved to make way for them, once they had passed, they quickly bent back into shape. The trees were unlike any the young girl had ever seen before; the branches seemed full of living light that darted off the moss in flashes of pink and purple.

After a few minutes, Otto came to an abrupt stop. In the moonlight, Antigone could see hundreds of stars reflected in water. They had arrived at the edge of a great lake. 'Fireflies black, use your might, help my sight and give me light,' Otto whispered into the dark. One by one, hundreds of fireflies appeared out of nowhere, each glowing individually, their tiny bodies beaming with a soft golden light so that Antigone could see Otto's face. 'I am sorry about earlier,' Otto said to Antigone. 'But I promise you are safe now. My name is Otto.'

Almost too stunned to speak, Antigone was bedazzled by the sight in front of her and took a moment to reply. 'My name is Antigone,' she said quietly. 'But what is this place? Where am I?' 'This is Lake Adamas, home of the fairies,' replied Otto. 'This is also my home.'

What lies beneath the waters is secret and known only to the fairies. At the bottom of the lake lie hundreds of thousands of gems – rubies, emeralds, sapphires and, most of all, diamonds – causing the lake's waters to flicker, shimmer and twinkle all day and night as if it were alive. On the other side of Lake Adamas is a giant glowing waterfall that cascades into the sparkling lake beneath it. Behind the waterfall is where all the fairies of Fandye live and, at the foot of the fairy waterfall, under the branches of a giant silver weeping willow, sits Señor Magic. This sleepy gnome is many hundreds

of years old and he is the protector of all the gems of Adamas. Antigone turned to Otto, her eyes wide with amazement. 'I've never seen anything like this before,' she exclaimed. 'This is my favourite place in Fandye,' replied Otto with a gentle smile. Antigone looked over to see the snoring Señor Magic asleep by the waterfall entrance. Two young fairies tugged and tickled his moustache, causing his top lip to twitch, but the old gnome remained fast asleep. Otto reached out his hand to Antigone, 'Come with me,' he whispered. 'But be quiet, we mustn't disturb Señor Magic, he can be a little grumpy.'

The pair crept past the sleeping gnome who let out an enormous snore, whistling as he exhaled. Behind the waterfall was a giant cavern; a city of fairies, each of whom had their own burrow-dwelling carved out of the rock wall. The lights from the gems still shimmered and twinkled behind the roaring wall of the glowing waterfall and, as Antigone looked up, she saw hundreds of fairies waking from their sleep, each one fascinated by her presence. The tiny creatures yawned and rubbed the sleep from their eyes as they peered out of their burrow-dwellings to get a better look at the passing wishmaker. Some let out little gasps and all looked on as their friend Otto guided her towards the back of the cavern to the largest fairy burrow-dwelling of them all.

Gliding through the sky towards Otto and Antigone flew Onya, Queen of the Fairies. About the size of a hummingbird and with delicate wings like a dragonfly, the Fairy Queen wore a tiny white gown with a golden crown perched on top of her flowing white hair. Queen Onya was the kindest and most respected fairy in Fandye. Antigone stood silent and still as the Fairy Queen hovered an inch from her face, inspecting her with great intrigue. The young girl watched transfixed as the beautiful fairy flew in front of her, the flutter of her little wings the only sound she could hear. After a few moments, Queen Onya closed her eyes and reached out her arm, placing her tiny hand on Antigone's nose. She held her hand there for some time, assessing the wishmaker. At first, she seemed shocked, but then she smiled, opened her eyes once again and looked directly at the young girl. Onya had understood something about the wishmaker that no one else knew.

One thing you must know about the fairies in Fandye is that their voices are so quiet that, just like a ladybird's whisper, they are almost impossible to hear. But the fairies were Otto's family, so he alone could understand them.

'Queen Onya would like me to tell you that you will be safe here,' Otto told Antigone. 'The fairies and I will ensure that none of the evil creatures of Fandye will ever find you.' Antigone looked at Otto. 'Thank you,' she said, 'but I must know, what are these evil creatures?' 'There are many out there,' replied Otto. 'But none you need to worry about tonight, you are safe here, Antigone. Now you must get some sleep.'

CHAPTER FOURTEEN

Antigone awoke early the next morning and for a few moments she thought it might have all been but a dream, and that she was back in bed at Gorwel Castle in Cornwall. But then, from far away, a haunting operatic melody floated through the dawn, and she knew it was all very real.

Upon opening her eyes Antigone saw that hanging by the entrance to the Fairy Queen's burrow-dwelling was an exquisite white dress. The beautiful gown twinkled just like an early morning spider's web glistening with pearly droplets of dew. Overnight, the fairies had spun the gown for Antigone from the threads of hundreds of midnight silkworms. Six fairies flew over to where Antigone had been sleeping, carrying the dress to her in the tips of their tiny fingers, leaving in their wake a glittering golden trail of fairy dust.

Antigone couldn't believe the fairies had made the beautiful dress just for her. She raised her arms above her head so they could slip it over her shoulders and then tie the ribbon in a bow behind her. 'Thank you so much,' Antigone said to the fairies, as she turned to see her reflection in the back of the cascading waterfall. 'It's the most beautiful dress I have ever seen in my whole life.' The fairies were thrilled with their creation and danced in delight, spinning and circling in the air around Antigone's head.

The haunting operatic melody started once again, far off on the winds of Fandye. 'Otto, wake up,' called Antigone, as she went to find her new friend, who was sleeping on a bed of reeds at the foot of the Fairy Queen's burrow-dwelling. 'Can you hear that sound?' she whispered to Otto as he was waking. 'I've heard it before somewhere.' 'That is no usual sound,' replied Otto, as he climbed up out of his bed. 'These are dark times in Fandye, Antigone, and that is the sound of an Opera-Singing Whale in distress. Opera-Singing Whales are the most majestic creatures in the waters of Fandye and to harm one is a terrible sin. Change is happening here; evil is looming and there have been whispers all around the islands that one of the Opera-Singing Whales has vanished. Ever since then, the callings have been getting louder and louder every night.' The fairies also listened to Otto and nodded their tiny heads in agreement.

'What evil is here, Otto?' asked Antigone in a frightened tone. 'I mustn't say too much, for he has spies everywhere,' whispered Otto, looking around with caution. 'But a terrible, monstrous beast lives in a cave on the top of the highest, darkest mountain in Fandye. His name is Sorlax. And he has an army of evil winged creatures who spend their time hunting on the horizon for children's wishes to feast on. They are called the Bumpindanites and it is this evil that we need to protect you from.'

Antigone was gripped and also terrified by what Otto was telling her. But she couldn't stop thinking about the operatic creatures whose voices haunted her. 'Tell me more about the whales,' she whispered to Otto. 'Many hundreds of years ago, Opera-Singing Whales were hunted for their blubber which was then burned down and made into oil,' he replied. 'Although this practice has now stopped, the last of the precious oil still exists.

It is said that when the oil is lit, an aurora of light bursts forth into fantastical colours that hypnotises anyone who sees it. This oil is so powerful, it is even said to penetrate the gates to the entrance of Fandye, as Opera-Singing Whales are the only creatures who can swim under the horizon.'

Antigone's mind flashed back to her bedroom at Gorwel Castle, to the lantern, to her aunt, to the darting colours, the boat and her journey towards the multi-coloured lights on the horizon. Suddenly it all made sense, she thought. 'Otto, will you please take me to see the whales?' Antigone asked softly. Otto paused. 'I am not sure Antigone, you are not safe on these islands,' he replied. 'Please Otto, I think I might be able to help,' she pleaded.

It probably wasn't the wisest move, nor one that would have made sense to you and I, but you have to remember that Otto and Antigone were both still very young and curious, so adventure was at the forefront of their minds.

Guided by the fireflies, they crept out from behind the waterfall, past the snoring Señor Magic and out into the dawn light. Down through the Forest of Pendragon, through the parting trees, and past the sleeping river pixies they ran, all the way to the Beach of the Never-Setting Sun.

The beach was empty, but the cry of the Opera-Singing Whales had become louder. Large waves crashed onto the sand, creating a giant stretch of ocean foam along the shore. As the waves repeatedly hit the beach, Antigone saw a ghostly line of white horses galloping onto the land. The waves got closer and closer to Antigone and Otto and so too the horses, their misty hooves thudding and pounding the wet sand before disappearing and fading into mist. Antigone stared, bewildered by the cloudy, phantom-creatures as they cantered down the beach. After a few moments, she noticed one prominent horse break away from the stampede. Standing well over five hands taller than the rest, and with a jet-black coat, an enormous winged stallion of the sea gracefully approached Antigone and Otto. As he galloped along the beach, his shiny coat glistened. The horse stopped, towering over both Antigone and Otto, and the little girl looked deep into the creature's dark eyes.

'I am Gee, the ruler of the waves,' said the winged stallion. 'And you, young wishmaker Antigone, are in very grave danger.' Antigone was stunned by the talking creature. 'How do you know my name?' she asked. 'There is no creature in Fandye who does not know your name,' replied Gee. 'News that a wishmaker has travelled across the horizon has spread all around the islands and, although I come in peace, there are those under the command of Sorlax who are hunting for you. I am afraid they will not stop until they have brought you to their dark ruler.'

'But what do they want from me?' asked Antigone. 'Your wishes,' Gee replied. 'A human wishmaker's wish is the most powerful charm in all of Fandye. If a blank wish were to be extracted from you and stolen – and I sincerely hope this does not happen – it could be used to grant the wish thief whatever they so desire. In the wrong hands, your wishes could be used for evil and darkness could well take over the islands. The lantern that brought you here may have opened the gates to the horizon, but it will not work again. The Opera-Singing Whale oil's magic is weakened now and is powerless to open the horizon gates once again. Therefore, it is of vital importance, Antigone, that you stay hidden and leave to go back home over the horizon at the very next eclipse.'

Antigone listened in fear. 'But why can I not wish now

to go back home across the horizon?' she asked Gee. 'If you do that, young girl, then all the evil creatures who are searching for you will most definitely find you. For if you were to make a wish in Fandye, your wish will glow as it heads up into the sky and will therefore alert those who are looking for you as to where you are. So, you must not make any wishes whilst you are on these islands, otherwise it is guaranteed you will be caught by any number of dark creatures because your wishes are of great value to them.'

Otto then turned to Antigone. 'I am afraid Gee is right,' he said. 'This is why I have been telling you that you are not safe here Antigone. But there is a place I know where we can hide.'

Suddenly a thick grey fog filled the air, rolling off the sea and creeping in through the forest of Pendragon. 'The fog is here! You must leave now!' bellowed Gee, as he rapidly disappeared from sight into the dense grey cloud descending on the beach. 'What is wrong with the fog?' Antigone asked, confused. 'The fog is the eyes and the ears of Sorlax and the Bumpindanites,' said a panicked Otto. 'We must run!'

Quickly they ran back through the Forest of

Pendragon, through the parting trees and all the way over to the other side of the island. Otto stopped at the foot of an ancient lone tree at the edge of the forest, whose enormous branches towered over them and curled forth like witches' fingers. Creeping vines curled their way around the tree's trunk and, in-between the vines, magnificent bright pink flowers bloomed.

At the base of the tree, there was a large hole in the trunk, around three feet tall, where lightning had once struck. 'Watch,' Otto said, as he bent down and climbed into the hole. The last thing Antigone saw were Otto's bare feet sticking out before he completely disappeared. 'Otto!' she called out into the silence.

After a few moments, Otto's hand popped out of the hole and he beckoned to Antigone. She placed her hand in his and climbed into the tree. They crept through a dark tunnel which came out to reveal a whole world, twenty times bigger than it looked from the outside. The tree was alive with activity and all around Antigone was the buzzing of moths. 'This is the Tree of the Goliath Hummingbird Moths,' Otto told her. A whole colony of moths the size of pigeons, painted in reds and pinks and blue, were busily working away storing pollen, their sticky tongues darting rapidly in and out of their mouths.

A single stream of dusty light beamed down from the very top of the tree. Hanging from the bark walls was a rope ladder made of slats of wood held together with strong reeds. Otto led the way, climbing up, up, up to the top of the tree. Antigone followed for what seemed like forever. The beam of dusty light got brighter and brighter the higher they climbed. Eventually, they arrived at the very top of the ladder and Otto helped Antigone up out of the trunk and onto the forest canopy. A mesh of vines and giant leaves spread out in front of them, like a bright green blanket covering the very top of the forest. Ahead of them was a spectacular view of the whole of Fandye – the Beaches of the Never-Rising and Never-Setting Sun, the terrifying dark snowy peak of Shadow Mountain, the Colossal Tortoises roaming through the dandelions of the Great Clear and, occasionally, the soft haunting call of the Opera-Singing Whales echoing all around them.

'Otto, I never believed in magic until I came here,' whispered Antigone. 'Do you think that magic is only in Fandye?' replied Otto with a questioning smile. 'I can tell you, Antigone, that while it might not always be obvious, trust me when I say that magic is always all around you, even in your world.' Antigone turned to look out once again at the spectacle in front of her. 'Otto, please tell me everything about the magic of Fandye.'

For the next hour or two, Otto explained all the magical secrets of the lands beyond the horizon. He told Antigone of the Flying Fish Footmen and the dodo's nesting grounds; of the silver-lining-makers in the northern lakes and the fierce men of Mount Catapult whose job it is to shoot lost stars back up into the night. And beyond all of this, Otto also told her more about the dangerous, dark magic in Fandye, of the evil of Sorlax and the Bumpindanites.

Antigone watched out from the canopy as shooting stars filled the sky, she saw the sea shimmer and, far off in the distance, the shadowy mass of Bumpindanites hunting for wishes on the horizon. By now, Otto and Antigone had been awake for hours. The young boy yawned, his eyelids heavy with sleep and he wrapped himself up under a giant leaf to rest. But Antigone couldn't sleep, her mind was racing with all that she had learnt and all that lay in front of her.

Suddenly, the haunting operatics of the whales

started once again, crying their now familiar plea. But this time, Antigone felt it was louder and more pained than before. She listened intently, looking out to sea in the direction of where the calls were coming from. Far off in the distance, Antigone could see the patch of broken water where the enormous creatures were breaking the surface with their dorsal fins.

Not for the first time on this adventure, some might consider that what Antigone did next to be very foolish indeed. It was also to dramatically alter the course of our story. For had the curious young girl stayed up with Otto, sleeping in the safety of the canopy, she may well have ended up back in the human world and escaped all the dangers of Fandye. But, well, it didn't quite turn out like that...

Instead, Antigone ignored the warnings of both Otto and Gee. She was determined to discover the cause of the Opera-Singing Whales' torment. Without waking Otto, she tiptoed over the vines, back down the rope ladder inside the Tree of Goliath Hummingbird Moths and out into the Forest of Pendragon. She ran alone through the parting trees, illuminated by the fireflies, past the river pixies and the great Lake Adamas until, once again, she reached the Beach of the Never-Setting

Sun.

Antigone spotted the bow of her little boat poking out from the mangrove in the very place where she and Otto had left it hidden. Using all her strength, she tugged the boat free from the creeping ivy and dragged it across the beach to the sea. The hem of her beautiful, sparkling fairy dress skimmed the shallow water as she climbed into the little boat. She reached for the wooden oars, pushed herself off the beach and sailed towards the call of the Opera-Singing Whales.

As she sailed away from the shore, the ocean mirrored the never-setting sun on the horizon, its orange glow beaming out like a fiery golden orb. After sailing for some time, the waters started to stir and Antigone's little boat rocked from side to side. Just ahead of her, she could see the whales; ten, maybe fifteen, all breaching above the water, chanting their now deafening cry. Their enormous tails, some eight feet wide, rose up, splashing through the ocean. Antigone looked on, spellbound by the magnificent creatures. One by one the whales then descended back down into the deep, until they disappeared from Antigone's sight altogether, leaving behind only a flat glassy sheet of water where their vast bodies had just been.

A few moments later, a giant spray of mist exploded from beneath the water, blasting high up into the air. Antigone was startled as the smallest of the pod of Opera-Singing Whales exhaled right next to her. The whale rose up next to the boat and its giant eye met Antigone's. In that moment, the little girl recognised the very same desperation and sadness in the creature as she had seen only days earlier on the banks of the River Thames in London. All the memories of that day came flooding back into her mind: the photographers, the news crews, the helicopters hovering above, but most of all, the intensity of the beached, dying whale's eye looking directly back at her.

Antigone suddenly remembered the radio in her aunt's kitchen at Gorwel Castle at breakfast time and the BBC news reader's report about how the whale in the River Thames had been an unidentified species. She then recalled how Otto had told her about the disappearance of an Opera-Singing Whale in Fandye. As she looked deep into the young whale's eye, she once again felt that unknown magical connection pass between them, and she knew without question that this was the baby of the whale that died in the River Thames.

The baby whale and the rest of the pod had been calling in distress for the missing mother and Antigone felt desperately sad for the creatures, as she alone knew what fate had befallen the mammal in the human world and understood how painful life without parents can be. Antigone slowly reached out to gently touch the whale's head. Its skin was the same silky, rubbery texture she had felt when she touched its mother just days earlier. All of a sudden, the baby whale let out a deafening, anguished cry, before lowering its head back under the sea and diving back down into the deep. The ocean turned completely still and no longer could Antigone hear the whales' operatics, instead the air had become deathly quiet all around her. Antigone looked around for a sign of the whales, but every one of them had now disappeared.

For the first time since crossing the horizon, Antigone felt very alone. With only the stars shining down on her for company, the little girl now deeply regretted leaving the sanctuary of the forest canopy and Otto. Antigone started to shiver and looked around the boat for some warmth, but there was nothing. She looked down into the ocean and all she could see were the stars and her own face mirrored in the still, quiet waters.

But Antigone was no longer alone. In the reflection, a razor-sharp talon suddenly appeared at her shoulder, followed by two faces of what can only be described as pure and utter evil. Their fanged teeth drooled as their grotesque features broke out into sinister smiles. They had found their prize. The beasts pounced on Antigone. Her beautiful sparkling fairy dress was ripped by their claws. Behind them a swarm of fellow Bumpindanites started screeching and hissing with delight as Antigone was grabbed from her boat by the two giant winged monsters. Antigone's screams echoed through Fandye, as she was carried far, far up into the sky and towards the dark peak of Shadow Mountain.

CHAPTER FIFTEEN

Antigone struggled in the grasp of the Bumpindanites' talons, their clawed feet piercing through both shoulders of her sparkling dress. The little girl was utterly terrified. Ahead of her, she could see the rugged mountaintop home of the Bumpindanites. Antigone's bare feet dangled in the freezing air as the Bumpindanites circled closer and closer to the crown of the mountain, their squeals and hisses echoing all around her. Below them, the wind swirled, causing tiny tornadoes at the entrance to Sorlax's lair. Into the cave they swooped and Antigone suddenly found herself in a vast, freezing cavern. She looked up to see hundreds of petrified fairies trapped in glass jars lighting the dank, wet walls. Below the fairy lights were giant tanks of wondrous-looking glowing fish of the deep, their bulging eyes blinking out into the stinking cave.

Antigone was dragged down the fairy-lit passageway, towards a terrifying noise. The tunnel opened up into an enormous amphitheatre in the round, a courtroom full of hundreds of rows of Bumpindanites, all hissing, spitting, biting and speaking to each other in their own language. As Antigone and her captors arrived from a door to the side of the sandy-floored pit, the courtroom immediately fell silent. From their courtside seats, the winged monsters peered down, jostling and pushing in front of one another to see what had entered the auditorium. Antigone covered her face in fear as the two beasts dropped her into the centre. Once in the middle of the pit, the two Bumpindanites stood back to reveal their prize. The courtroom erupted in mass hysteria as the beasts realised that the much-anticipated wishmaker had been captured. Cackles and screams of celebration filled the amphitheatre as Antigone stood up, trembling in her tattered white fairy dress, to see the hundreds of half-bat, half-human creatures looking down on her, their fanged faces glowing red, illuminated by giant candles.

Inside, Antigone had never been so scared in all her

life, but she was a brave young girl and she didn't let her fear show through on the outside. The deafening thud of giant footsteps suddenly echoed through the auditorium and the Bumpindanites' hysteria subsided as they cowered in their seats, awaiting the arrival of their master.

The shadow of the nine-foot monster loomed at the entrance to the courtroom, with his ever-present servant Intoku by his side. Sorlax slowly approached Antigone and the little girl looked up, speechless and open-mouthed, as he towered over her.

'Hello wishmaker,' Sorlax said in his dark, sinister

tones. 'I haven't seen a wishmaker in so long, I had almost forgotten what you looked like.' He came closer to Antigone until the stench of his revolting breath filled the air around her.

'Let me tell you a secret,' the monster continued. 'Many hundreds of years ago, I was a wishmaker, a human just like you, but I was not a very nice one. And once I died, I didn't go where others may go, I became what I am now. And this,' he said, gesturing towards all the hundreds of seething Bumpindanites filling the courtroom, 'is my army. We are the things that you daren't dream of when you lie awake at night. We are the creeks downstairs, the eyes in the wardrobe and the rattling of the window panes.'

Antigone raised her head and looked directly at Sorlax. 'What am I doing here, you monster?' she asked him, and then, 'Are you going to hurt me?' Her question prompted the entire courtroom to erupt into shrieks of laughter. 'Silence!' bellowed Sorlax, while also chuckling to himself at the girl's suggestion. 'No, I am not going to hurt you, not too much, anyway,' he responded. 'You are far too important to me, young Antigone. For in Fandye, a child's blank wish is the most powerful enchantment. By stealing a blank wish from you, I can use it to ask the stars for whatever I desire.'

Antigone trembled, but did not let her fear betray her. 'It is a dreadful thing to steal a blank wish from a child,' Sorlax continued. 'In doing that, I will be taking a part of your soul and your happiest childhood memories – the first smile your parents ever gave you or the feeling of holding your father's hand – all will be forgotten.'

Sorlax extended two of his long, grey, bony fingers towards Antigone's mouth and, with his thumb and forefinger pinched together, he began the slow and painful process of extraction. Suddenly Antigone's whole body froze and she found herself unable to move as her mouth was prized open by the monster. Her eyes darted around in fear as slowly Sorlax started to tug from inside her mouth and a long stream of childhood memories came flowing out, like a ribbon of magical cinematic film reel.

Once again, the Bumpindanites started yelping and shrieking with delight as they watched their master carry out the most evil form of all Fandye sorcery. 'Intoku, the bottle, now!' snapped Sorlax, as his servant pulled a glass jar from inside his cape and quickly handed it to his master. Sorlax carefully threaded the wish ribbon into the glass jar and bottled it with a cork. He held the bottle close up to his face and observed the blank wish whizzing and flashing around inside the jar.

All the colour had drained from Antigone's face and her limbs were weak and limp. 'Young Antigone, with this blank wish, you have granted me all I that I have ever desired and with this I plan to...'

But before Sorlax got a chance to finish his sentence, he was interrupted by a fanfare of thousands of fluttering wings and the courthouse was suddenly invaded by a dazzle of fairies. They entered from every portal, followed by Otto riding on the back of Gee, the Stallion King of the Sea.

The entire fairy kingdom of Lake Adamas had flown to Shadow Mountain to rescue Antigone and, upon arriving at Sorlax's cave, they had used their magic to free all their captured fairy friends, smashing them out of their small glass prisons.

Although tiny in size, the flock of fairies far outnumbered the Bumpindanites and an almighty fight broke out. The Bumpindanites took flight from their seats in the courthouse and swarmed in the air towards the oncoming fairies. But before they had a chance to attack, an allegiance of the tiny magical creatures ambushed the Bumpindanites with a rainbow of sparkling fairy dust that sprinkled down and blinded the monsters who all screeched and hissed in agony.

Down below on the sandy courthouse floor, a panicked Sorlax held the wish bottle tightly in his bony hands. He turned his back on the fairies and escaped back to his chambers. Otto rode over to where Antigone was now slumped in the middle of the amphitheatre. Gee bent down and Otto jumped off the stallion and ran towards his friend. 'Antigone, I am so sorry,' said Otto. 'This should never have happened, I feel this is all my fault.' He helped the little girl stand on her feet and climb up onto the back of Gee. 'We need to get her to safety,' said Otto to the stallion. 'King Archon is the only one who can help us now, we must fly!'' Gee bowed his head, 'You are right young Otto, the royalty of Fandye is our only hope.'

Holding the near unconscious Antigone tightly on the back of Gee, Otto rode the Stallion King out of the courthouse, down the dark tunnel and into the freezing air. Outside on the cliff edge, Gee opened his enormous wings and galloped off into the sky, heading for the palace of Fandye.

CHAPTER SIXTEEN

On the highest cliff within the palace of Fandye lies a beautiful, grand courtyard surrounded by impcccably manicured lawns, ornate hedges and enchanting gardens. In the very centre of the courtyard sits an enormous fountain from which cascades the most magnificent display. The waters of the fountain are alive with hundreds of miniature mermaids the size of seahorses, all quietly swimming, diving and dancing in the surrounding pools. At one end of the courtyard stands a formation of tens of marble statues of the previous Kings and Queens of Fandye all dressed in their regal finery.

Apart from the gentle splashing of the mermaids' tails, and the soft whistling of the wind, it was silent when the large shadow of the winged stallion landed on the terrace. Carrying the precious cargo of the young boy and girl, Gee walked slowly towards the fountain and lowered his body to allow Otto and Antigone to climb down onto the marble floor. The girl, who had just started to regain her strength, dismounted and stared up at the enormous palace with its turrets and gargoyles towering over her.

Behind two giant doors at the far end of the terrace, the clicking of steel-capped boots marching along polished floors could be heard. The doors suddenly swung open and in front of the visitors stood the lone figure of King Archon. 'Who goes there?' enquired the King, who was visibly nervous at the strangers' invasion of his palace. Gee, the Stallion King of the Sea, raised his head and responded, 'Your Majesty, my friend, you need not fear, it is only I, Gee. 'And who is with you, Sea Stallion?' asked Archon, still suspicious of the uninvited guests.

'I am with Otto of Lake Adamas, Sire, and his friend, who is a wishmaker from beyond the horizon.' Archon's eyes widened. 'You have the wishmaker?' he asked in disbelief. The King slowly walked out of the doorway and towards Antigone. 'Yes, Your Majesty, and we need your help,' responded Gee. 'You, Sire, are the only person we can trust to protect the young wishmaker.'

Now, you must remember that in all the years that had passed since the young Archon lost his love to the horizon, the King had become a very different man altogether. A recluse from most of his kingdom, he had become anxious, weak and a shadow of his former self. Since striking the evil deal with Sorlax and sacrificing all his kingly powers, his face had become gaunt and his skin sallow. He was almost unrecognisable from the man he had once been. The King was now standing in front of the young girl, who was clinging on to Otto.

'Where have you come from, young wishmaker?' asked Archon. Antigone remained silent, her head bowed, still weak from the trauma of what had just happened to her. 'We rescued her from Shadow Mountain where she had been captured by Sorlax and his army, Your Majesty,' explained Otto. 'However, I am afraid we were too late,' added Gee. 'And by the time we arrived, the monster had already extracted a wish from the child.'

Archon walked even closer to Antigone and crouched down in front of the girl to inspect her. Antigone looked up and spoke for the first time, her voice laced with quiet desperation. 'Your Majesty, please will you help us,' she asked the King.

But Archon's mind had started to race; if Sorlax had stolen a wish, then why couldn't he? Then he could ask for the immediate return of his lost love from beyond the horizon which would be guaranteed by the stars.

'Young wishmaker, I would very much like to help you,' responded Archon as he stood back up and looked down upon the weak young girl pleading with him. For a moment, the King was unsure what to do. It would have been all too easy not to harm her and to simply lock the palace gates and keep the Bumpindanites far away until the next eclipse. But the King's obsession was all-consuming, his mind infected with selfish desire. And as much as his head told him that he should not steal a wish and hurt the little girl, it was his broken heart that led him: he needed his love back.

'But I am afraid, if I am to keep you safe,' the King said, 'I need something from you, child, in return... I need one of your wishes.' Gee, in sudden panic, shouted out, 'Your Majesty, you cannot! With all due respect, your true self knows the effect of such action. This dark magic should never be used! I cannot allow it!' The stallion reared and spread his wings in an attempt to shield Antigone, but Archon had already grasped hold of her arm and was pulling the girl into his clutches. He pointed his fingers towards her open mouth to start the extraction. Antigone tried to scream, but no sound came out. Once again, the young girl's whole body froze on the spot, as Archon began the painful process of the wish extraction.

As Gee continued to cry out in protest, suddenly a gust of ice-cold air blasted through the turrets of the palace and freezing fog started rolling through the courtyard. The flap of giant wings could be heard echoing all around the turrets, as a silhouette of pure evil passed the moon. Sorlax landed in the middle of the terrace, followed shortly afterwards by his loyal servant Intoku. The monster lowered his wings and stood towering over the King.

'Good evening, Your Majesty, so I see you've found our wishmaker,' said Sorlax.

Archon tightened his hold on Antigone, who remained frozen and unable to move. 'And what do we have here?' the monster enquired. 'Surely the good King Archon is not planning to steal a wish from the child?' Sorlax started laughing to himself. 'This is

none of your business, stay away from the wishmaker!'
bellowed Archon, as he tried to continue the extraction.
'Oh, do be quiet,' Sorlax hissed to the King. 'It is not
the wishmaker I am here for, I have everything I need
from her. No, I am here for you.' A sinister smile crept
across the monster's face. 'What could you possibly
need from me now, beast?' Archon asked angrily.
Sorlax laughed again, only this time louder.

Suddenly through the fog came a piercing screech
– the Bumpindanites were on their way from across
the horizon. 'Soorlaaaax,' they hissed triumphantly,
their callings carried on the winds. Four beasts led the
pack as they approached the palace and, dangling from
their talons, was a large green fishing net containing
the figure of a woman. The assembled crowd looked up
and watched as the Bumpindanites circled the palace's
turrets. They hissed and screeched in delight before
they swooped down to the courtyard and dropped the
prize at their master's feet. The net collapsed to reveal
a familiar blonde lady wearing a pink silken dress. The
Bumpindanites had finally found and captured King
Archon's lost love.

With the net at her ankles, Lavinia looked over to
see the terrified young girl in the grasp of King Archon.

She scrambled to her feet and shouted out to the King, 'No Archon, you must not harm her!' Archon looked up in complete shock. 'Lavinia?' he uttered, unable to believe his eyes. It had been almost thirteen years since Archon had lost Lavinia to the horizon and here she was standing in front of him in his palace. This was the very moment he had been waiting for every day since he watched her sail across that misty line; the moment he'd dreamt of and obsessed over and ultimately sacrificed all his kingly powers for.

As the King's eyes turned towards his lost love, the wish extraction spell was broken and the magical connection lost. Antigone gasped and, using all her strength, prized herself free from the arms of Archon and started running towards the woman. 'Aunt Lavinia?!' Antigone cried, with tears streaming down her face. 'I can't believe you are here! I'm so sorry, I should never have left you!' She threw her arms around Lavinia. 'My dear child, I too am so sorry, I should have told you the truth a long time ago,' Lavinia said as she held Antigone in her arms. 'I have tried to keep you safe and far away from Cornwall, because I knew deep down that the powers of Fandye would one day try to pull you across the horizon, just as they did me. You must know, my darling, that I have been here before. It was many years ago, just before you were born. I got lost in a storm and sailed through the gates of Fandye during an eclipse and I got rescued. And I fell in love. But I could not stay.'

Lavinia stopped for a moment and turned to look lovingly towards Archon. 'When I came back home across the horizon, I knew that I was expecting a baby and every time I saw an eclipse I knew that you would be waiting for me to come back, Archon,' she said.

Lavinia then turned back to face Antigone, crouched down and took the young girl's hands into hers. 'But then you were born, Antigone, and the moment I saw you and your little hands glowed, I realised I loved you more than I had ever loved anything. That's why I decided never to return to Fandye and for you to live in the human world. So, I sent you to London, to live with a new family to be safe. I wanted you to lead the life of a normal little girl, far from the Bumpindanites and this magical world. But you must now know the truth, you are a princess in Fandye and I am your mother.' Lavinia then stopped, stood up and turned back towards the King: 'My darling Archon, she is your daughter.'

'Silence!' bellowed Sorlax. 'I do so hate to interrupt

this precious family reunion, but I am afraid, Archon, that it is my turn to share some news. You see, I have been dreaming of this day for as long as I can remember,' Sorlax continued. 'Because, Archon, your royal powers and your army of guards have always prevented me from getting what I truly desire. But now you have no power and you have no army. You may have brought your human love back to Fandye and you may have gained a daughter, but she is no true blood heir. She is of curdled blood, half-human and half-Fandye, a magical and human bond that does not blend to make a successor to the throne.' Sorlax turned to Antigone. 'You may have royal blood in your veins, child, and your hands may glow, but you have no power to be Queen, and your magic has only half-strength, not even enough to prevent me from killing your father.'

The monster reached under his wing and retrieved the bottle containing Antigone's stolen blank wish alive and darting inside the small glass container. He pulled out the cork and the wish unfurled as a magical roll of coloured tape, which he then pincered between his two bony fingers. 'I wish for King Archon to be dead!' Sorlax slowly whispered to the blank wish, before throwing it high up into the night sky to find

Antigone's star.

Upwards the wish soared, through the fog, past the gargoyles and over the turrets, until it reached its faraway star, which immediately exploded into light. In a startling flash, a dazzling beam struck down onto Archon, stopping the King's heart and killing him instantly. Lavinia let out an agonising cry as she ran over to the King's motionless body which had collapsed on to the cold marble at the foot of the fountain. Falling to the floor, she held his head close to her body and, with tears running down her face, she kissed him. 'I have never stopped loving you Archon,' she sobbed. 'Never a day went by when I didn't think about sailing back over the horizon to be with you...'

As Lavinia held her one true love in her arms and wept, Antigone, Otto and Gee congregated around the King in solemn silence. But Lavinia's cries were drowned out by the screeches of the Bumpindanites who were all celebrating King Archon's death, flying and swooping around the palace turrets in an excited frenzy.

'The King is dead!' Sorlax boomed as he marched over to where Lavinia sat cradling Archon in her arms. Then in one swipe of his skeletal arm he removed the

King's bejewelled golden crown from his head. Lavinia cowered as the monster spread his vast wings and, after placing the King's crown on his own head, he declared: 'I am the new King! I am the King of Fandye!' Then, addressing his new subjects, he demanded: 'Bow before your new King!'

Darkness filled the sky as every Bumpindanite in Fandye swarmed to the palace to pay homage to the new King Sorlax. Two of the beasts then grabbed hold of Lavinia and Antigone, dragging them away from Archon's body, and forced them to bow at Sorlax's feet. Gee and Otto looked at each other in horror. 'Bow to your new King!' repeated Sorlax in anger, turning to the stallion and the boy. 'I will never bow to you or your army,' Gee stated in defiance, but his words meant nothing. Two more Bumpindanites then ambushed Gee from above and pinned themselves to him, dragging their talons across his back until he fell to his knees in pain, in front of the new King of Fandye. Meanwhile, Otto, too terrified to disobey the new King, also obliged and bowed to Sorlax.

The evil King stood and surveyed the crowd and he knew that the only task left to complete his transformation was to drink the royal powers. He summoned his most loyal courtier, Intoku. 'Give me the bottle of the dead King's royal powers, servant!' Sorlax demanded.

Intoku raised his head and reached inside his cape to salvage the precious bottle. But he stopped and did not hand it over to his master. For he knew the truth.

After three hundred years of working as a slave to Sorlax, witnessing his every evil deed, he realised he was now no longer scared of the consequences of his actions. 'No, Sorlax,' Intoku said calmly as he met his master's eye. 'They are not your powers to have.' Never before had Sorlax been challenged in such a way. 'Hand me the powers now! I will not ask again, fool!' he screamed, as rage started soaring through his veins

Intoku remained calm. 'You are not the King,' he said, as he stared straight into his master's eyes. The Bumpindanites started to growl and snarl. 'Of course I am King,' Sorlax's fury echoed around the palace walls. 'Archon is dead! I am the King!' he said as he gestured towards Archon's corpse.

At that very moment, Intoku, who was standing next to Otto, turned his head and pointed to the boy. Speaking directly to Otto, in front of all assembled, he announced, 'You are the King.' He then produced the bottle of kingly powers from inside his cape. 'You, Otto, are the rightful heir to the throne of Fandye,' he continued. 'Thirteen years ago, a princess was captured and imprisoned on Shadow Mountain. She was expecting a baby, but sadly she died giving birth to him. Sorlax then ordered me to kill that child but, standing at the cliff's edge, looking down at the baby, I could not go through with it. So, I took the baby and hid it under my cloak whilst throwing the empty basket down to the rocks below. You were that baby, Otto. I then took you live with the fairies of Lake Adamas, who promised they would keep you safe behind the waterfall until you were old enough to know the truth. You are now the King and these powers belong to you.'

Sorlax roared, grabbed Intoku by the neck and lifted the dwarf off the floor. 'How dare you! You disobeyed me?' he screamed at his servant. 'I will kill you for this!' His talons tightened around Intoku's throat. At that moment, Intoku, struggling in Sorlax's grasp, threw the bottle of kingly powers to the floor. The glass shattered, releasing the golden smoke which swirled its way straight into Otto's mouth. The young boy looked down in wide-eyed amazement as his hands started to glow.

'I am the King?' Otto asked Intoku in disbelief, his whole body now sparkling as his kingly powers developed. All his life, the fairies of Lake Adamas had kept him safe as one of their own behind the waterfall, and all that time he had never understood where he came from. But now, with the powers inside him, he realised that this was his fate and that the future of Fandye now lay in his hands.

Stunned by the events that had just taken place, Sorlax suddenly took several steps back, as he realised that Otto's powers were now far greater than his own.

With his arms outstretched and glowing, Otto looked the monster directly in the eyes. 'You killed my family and you ordered my death, you do not deserve to live, Sorlax,' he warned him. He then dropped his hands in a gesture of peace and said: 'But if you and your army leave Fandye today and you promise never to return to these islands, then no harm will come to you.'

The new King Otto then turned his back on Sorlax and walked over to Antigone and Lavinia. But the monster had no intention of leaving, instead he started laughing. 'You can try to banish me, you can try to rid me of my army, you can even try and kill me, boy, but I am afraid that I am already dead,' Sorlax grinned at Otto. 'You can try to be noble, but this is a war between good and evil. And I will be King. I will haunt your sleep and I will hide in your shadow, waiting for any wrong move you might make. Your fate will be the same as Archon's – a young King whose weakness and stupidity was his ultimate downfall.' The monster then turned to address his army, 'The child King will be overturned!' he screamed. 'We will never leave Fandye! For we are, and always will be, the things that go bump in the night!'

Otto had tried to reason with the monster, but when it comes to monsters, as the new King would soon learn, there is no room for reasoning. And so, summoning all his newly anointed kingly powers, Otto turned back to face Sorlax and outstretched both his arms once again. This time, the powers started beaming from his palms and two shafts of light burst forth with sparks shooting and fizzing towards Sorlax.

The Bumpindanites took flight as their leader started to combust, smoking and sizzling on the palace courtyard, under the statues of the former Kings and Queens of Fandye. Then there was the most almighty, deafening boom as the nine-foot creature suddenly exploded into an enormous puff of dust. The King's golden crown remained suspended in the air for just a millisecond before falling and crashing to the ground. All that was left behind of Sorlax was a huge, black pile of ash on the white marble floor.

The events that happened that night in the courtyard of the Palace of Fandye have never been forgotten. The story has been re-told so many times, by so many hundreds of people over the years that it has now become the stuff of legend. There are many different versions told by magic folk on the other side of the horizon, but I promise you all that you have read so far is the absolute truth and I know, because I was there and I watched it all take place. And I also know what happened next to our young Antigone. The following day the little girl and her mother Lavinia were given, by royal decree, the gift of an Opera-Singing Whale. The very same whale that Antigone had met at sea, whose mother had died on the banks of the River Thames. Because, you see, the only thing more powerful than Opera-Singing Whale oil is when it is flowing through the veins of one of Fandye's most beautiful creatures. They are the only ones who have the power to open the gates to Fandye and travel under the horizon into the human world. And so, the little girl and her mother rode their way home to Cornwall on the back of the enormous whale.

But, shortly before they held their breath to go under the horizon, Antigone made two wishes. The first was for Otto to be a great and much-loved King and the second was for peace in Fandye. But I know something that Antigone does not. For at that very moment, just as the wishes were passing up through the clouds and heading towards the stars, out of nowhere one lone, hungry Bumpindanite appeared. The beast swooped down and swallowed up one of the little girl's two wishes, leaving only one to be granted by her star.

And as to what happened next? Well that, dear friend, is another story for another day.

THE END

ABOUT THE AUTHOR

Ollie Locke first found fame on Channel 4's BAFTA award-winning show, *Made In Chelsea*. Since then he has gone on to appear in over 40 television shows.

Ollie's 2013 autobiographical comedy *Laid In Chelsea*, ranked him in the top three of the Sunday Times Bestsellers.

The Islands of Fandye is Ollie's fictional debut, the first of a fairytale trilogy he started creating as a child whilst on family holidays in North Cornwall.

Ollie lives in West London with his fiance, Gareth, and their dog, Bear.

Printed in Great Britain
by Amazon